A HERO'S LIFE

By ARTHUR A. EDWARDS

A Hero's Life

A fighter pilot is faced with an impossible dilemma when he returns home from the war.

ISBN: 978-1-61170-220-0

Published by:

 Robertson Publishing™
www.RobertsonPublishing.com

Printed in the USA and UK on acid-free paper.

Author's Previous Novel:

War is Hell — ISBN 978-1-61170-190-6
A novel about war and its meaning to the men and women who fight it.

The author's books are available on:
amazon.com
barnesandnoble.com

Dedication

This book is dedicated to my cousin
and all of the other Air Force and Navy pilots
killed in
training accidents

First Lieutenant James Lyle Teeslink
Born March, 1929, Grand Junction, Colorado
Parents James and Evelyn Rice Teeslink
Lived in Oakland, California 1941 - 1951
Graduated University of California, Berkeley, 1951
Bachelor of Science, Business Administration
Enlisted in the U. S. Air Force 1951
Killed December 1954, at McChord Air Force base,
Tacoma, Washington

I also wish to offer my sincere thanks and deep appreciation to my editor and friend Donna Endacott. She offered encouragement when I needed it most, made timely suggestions and did valuable proof reading as I went along. This book would not exist if it were not for her.

I want to thank my wife, Shirley for her help and encouragement, and to my daughter, Diana, who always thought I should write. I am continually saddened that she did not live to see the results of her encouragement.

PROLOGUE

My cousin, Fist Lieutenant James Lyle Teeslink, an Air Force fighter pilot, was killed in a collision with his wingman over McChord Air Force base, Tacoma, Washington, in December 1954. They were both flying the F-86D Saber Jet. The Air Force investigating team ruled that the accident was caused by "pilot error," as one plane turned into the other. This conclusion struck me as being a cop-out because the Air Force either did not know the real cause or was unwilling to admit that there was something wrong with its prime fighter plane. Both pilots were experienced first lieutenants, were well trained and were unlikely to turn intentionally without telling his partner.

Consequently, I've often wondered about the accuracy of the Air Force's conclusion and have spent the years since 1954 searching for clues that would lead me to the real cause of the crash. During that time I read several articles and books that referred to a "faulty design" of the slats in the wing of the F-86.

A few months ago I talked with a local man who had flown the F-86 during the Korean War. It was his opinion that the plane was "dangerous to fly", and he told me that many pilots were killed in it. I then began searching the web and found a number of references to the problem with the F-86 wing slats and their operation. My new local friend flew the F-86 in Korea although the D model was never flown in combat. However, the wing slat design was apparently the same on all of the early models of the F-86.

He told me that it was his opinion that the Air Force and the plane's manufacturer had both known about the problem since the late 1940's but had not fixed it. I have been unable to confirm this and have read no books that stated why the wing slats might have malfunctioned. However, there is considerable discussion about the problem in Wikipedia and I can find nothing to contradict the fact that a problem existed.

This book is a fictional account of an aerospace engineer who identified a problem with the country's prime fighter plane and then has to decide if he should "blow the whistle," on the plane or let it remain in service.

Jimmie and I built model airplanes together during WW II and agreed that we would both be pilots, he in the Air Force and I in the Navy. He was the best man in my wedding but he never married. I became a line Navy officer, but did not fly.

As a retired aerospace engineer, I've often wondered what I would do if I discovered a design flaw in an important fighter plane or satellite. Maybe I would react the way the hero in my book does. Maybe I would not.

When I started to write this story I had no idea how it would end. In any case, I hope the reader enjoys this fictional account of what was apparently a real problem that existed in our country's best fighter plane. Maybe you will ask yourself, "What would I do under similar circumstances?"

The picture of a handsome twenty-five year old pilot climbing into the cockpit of his fighter jet you see on the cover of this book was taken less that a week before Jimmie was killed.

CHAPTER ONE

"Mr. Pritchard, Mr. Stern's secretary just called and he would like you to attend a meeting in his conference room right away. I think you should straighten your tie and put your coat on." Louise, his private secretary, smiled as she turned to walk out of his office. She was always working for his interests and tried hard to make him look his best whenever the occasion required. Steve didn't pay much attention to how he looked, except when he wore his Air Force uniform. He had spent long enough looking sharp for the general's inspection, and now he was going to kick back and look as sloppy as he could get away with.

"So what in the devil does our company president, want with me?" He asked his secretary. She shrugged. His thoughts wandered over everything he had done recently as he put slide rule away and his coat on, but couldn't think of anything he should get chewed out for. As he walked by his secretary's desk, he looked down and asked, "Louise, did she tell you what this meeting is about?"

"No Sir, Janet didn't say".

Janet was Mr. Stern's administrative assistant and was as much in charge of the company as was Mr. Stern. She was not one to be trifled with.

As Steve quickly walked up the stairs to the executive offices on the top floor, his section manager, John Chambers and then his division manager, Bill Johnson, joined him. Since they both had smiles on their faces as they walked up together, Steve assumed that the meeting wasn't going to be too bad after all.

They all stopped by Janet's desk to pay their respects, and she ushered them into the president's private conference room. Steve hadn't been there often, but he was always impressed with the plush chairs and beautiful pictures hanging on the wall. There were inevitably coffee and donuts available if anyone wanted them. No one, however, took a donut. They were all afraid that they would get crumbs on the president's shiny table.

A number of top executives walked in and sat around the table. All smiled and nodded at Steve. In a few minutes, Janet walked in, sat in a chair against the wall and opened her notebook. It would be her task to record everything that happened in the meeting. They all sat fidgeting and talking quietly to each other. After ten minutes or so, Mr. Stern walked in through his private entrance with a big smile on his face. Everyone stood up until he sat. Since Mr. Stern had been a general during the war, he rather liked the formality of employees standing when he entered the room.

"Welcome everybody and please help yourselves to coffee and donuts;" everyone smiled. One of the division leaders poured a cup of coffee. "I have not announced the purpose of this meeting because I wanted it to be a surprise, especially for the key member, Steve Pritchard." Mr. Stern looked at Steve with a big smile.

"This is a special occasion because Steve has solved a problem with the design of our transport, the C-145, that no one else had seen. As you all know, we had issues with parts of its fuselage tearing off when flying at high altitude.

2

The Air Force was naturally very concerned and threatened to cancel our contract. I asked Steve to take a look at the problem that he identified as being corrosion induced fatigue failure in the aluminum. For the benefit of those of you who aren't engineers, let me review the parameters of the problem."

Mr. Sterns was not an engineer himself but liked to think that he was able to understand technical issues that were routine problems for his engineering staff. It usually took several briefings for him to grasp the significance of what his staff was trying to tell him. This one was no exception.

"As you recall, various sections of skin would tear along the cabin section while the plane was in flight on those planes that had been in service the longest. Re-calculations by our engineering department confirmed that the stress loads were not, in themselves, sufficiently high to cause the failures. Something was happening that was unknown in aluminum fractures on airplanes.

"Fortunately, we had the right man for the job, Steve Pritchard, was given the task to pursue this brand new problem, never before seen in aircraft design. And he did pursue it, doggedly, until he identified the problem. Based on his work, we can assure our customer, the Air Force, that we have it all in hand, will modify all C-145's now in use, and can guarantee that the problem won't reappear in the future."

Mr. Stern sat back in his chair, folded his hands on his lap and showed a self-satisfied smile to all of his staff, including Steve. "Steve, why don't you tell us how you solved this problem?"

Steve looked around the room at the section heads and staff members who were now all looking at him in anticipation. How'd I get into this, he wondered?

"Well, It all started in the 1920's when the first airliner, the Ford Tri Motor, was built with aluminum skin rather than the cloth skins that were used on the fighter planes of World War I. The use of aluminum was brilliant because it is strong, light and is abundant in nature. It did the job with great success."

He paused to assemble his story. He felt some resentment because Mr. Stern had not warned him that he was going to make a presentation to his staff.

"Over the years, as you know, we have continued to use aluminum as skin material," he spoke slowly and deliberately, "Designing each application based on the stress calculations was done by the various engineering departments." He looked over at Ben Crawford, head of the company's design engineering department. Ben smiled back at him. They had worked together since Steve went to work with his company after the war.

"But there was one thing we didn't consider, the reduction of material strength do to fatigue stresses. The load a material can withstand due to fatigue loads is called endurance limit. We know that steel has an endurance limit, and we know when it will be reached. But aluminum has been used in airplanes only since the 1920's, so we were not expecting the loss in strength when we saw it. The failures occurred all along the rivet lines which one would expect, but the fractures looked nothing like anyone had seen before."

Now most of the people in the room were getting bored. Some looked at their watches, but Mr. Stern beamed with pride as the discussion continued. Consequently, everyone sat quietly trying to show interest.

"Would you explain to us what fatigue failure means, and how it differs from normal stress failure?" Ron McCabe was the head of purchasing who always tried to ask

4

relevant questions. He tried his best to express interest as he glanced at Mr. Stern out of the corners of his eyes.

"Sure," Steve responded. "The best example is to take a paper clip and straighten it out. Then bend it back and forth several times until it breaks. The first time you bend it nothing happens, but after several bends it breaks easily. This shows that metal looses strength by the process of applying and then releasing loads. This is called fatigue stressing.

"Our problem was that at first it did not appear that cabin skin was subjected to applied and then released stresses, but then I thought about the process of pressurizing the cabin at high altitudes. And that was no doubt the reason it happened on the C-145. It flies higher than any pressurized plane built until now. Consequently, as the plane climbs in altitude, the pressure on the outside drops while the cabin pressure inside is held near sea level for passenger comfort. Every time one of our C-145's flies somewhere, it goes up and comes down, a stress cycle on the skin of the airplane. After so many of these cycles, the skin begins to tear unperceptively along the rivet line and eventually rips off the plane. You've all seen the results of this skin failure."

Everyone sat quietly in the room waiting for someone to speak. "In any case," Mr. Stern said, "after Steve identified the problem our engineering department increased the skin thickness and provided supports in just the right places. The problem is now solved. And most importantly, our customer is very happy." Everyone clapped and smiled at Steve.

Mr. Stern reached down under the table. "So I would like to present this plaque to Steve as a token of our gratitude and respect for the great work he's done to save this company. There is also a raise and promotion coming that I will share with him in private.

Mr. Stern showed the trophy to everyone to the audible gasps and obvious approval of everyone present. When he finally brought it over to Steve and set it down in front of him, they shook hands and Mr. Stern gave Steve a pat on the back.

"Wow!" He had no trouble acting surprised. "I'm very appreciative and will keep this on my desk to remind me of the support I've received from all of you here." He knew he sounded a little corny.

As everyone clapped Mr. Stern rose as a signal that the meeting was over, and it was time for his staff to get back to work. "Please hang around Steve. I want to talk to you privately for a few minutes."

"Of course, Sir."

CHAPTER TWO

Everyone shook Steve's hand and offered congratulations as they walked out of the conference room. He finally turned around and sat back down across the table from the president. Mr. Stern pulled a piece of paper out of his briefcase and slid it over to Steve. "This will be your new salary."

Steve looked down at the paper, and a single number jumped off the page at him. "Wow. I don't know what to say."

"You deserve it, that's all that needs to be said." Mr. Stern smiled at Steve and reached for another piece of paper. "Your new job, as outlined in these papers is that of senior test pilot in charge of design problems. You and your department will be responsible to review all new designs and identify issues you spot. It'll be your responsibility to review designs and test prototype aircraft to identify design flaws and other problems, hopefully before they manifest themselves. When necessary, you will also assist customers in determination of failures in existing aircraft, inspecting crash sites and damaged aircraft for causes of failures." Mr. Stern paused to watch the expression on Steve's face.

Steve was obviously shaken be the extent of his new

responsibilities. It was one thing to search out and identify one design problem as he had done. But to be in charge of the department that had such a continuing responsibility was beyond his imagination.

"I—am without words. Thank you very much Sir for your expression of confidence. I indeed hope that I'm worthy of your support." Steve could think of nothing else to say.

Mr. Stern smiled. "Now here's your first task in your new job. You may want to take notes." Steve opened up his notebook and took out his pen.

"As you know, our new F-87 Air Force fighter has had a troubling start since its deployment last March. There have been several instances in which control was lost in flight causing the plane to crash killing their pilots. You may have heard that in none of the cases has the Air Force been able to identify the cause of the problem. They've asked for our assistance." He paused to let his words sink in. Steve nodded.

"In each case, upon inspection, the aircraft has shown to be in perfect condition, including those that have crashed. You have heard about the latest incident that happened last week when two F-87's collided shortly after take off at McChord Air Force base in Tacoma, Washington. The witnesses say that one of the planes, the wingman from the description, suddenly rolled into the other causing both planes to crash in flames. The Air Force concluded that it was 'pilot error' that caused the wingman to turn too soon. The case is closed as far as they are concerned."

Steve remembered that he had heard of the incident, but since he was finishing up his final report on the skin failure on his company's troop carrier, he didn't follow the news on the investigation. "So if the case is closed, what do you want me to do?"

8

"There have been several critical newspaper reports saying that there is something wrong with our F-87 that is causing these crashes, and that we are trying to cover up the problem to avoid embarrassment. I want you to follow-up now with a trip up to Tacoma, see what you can find at the crash scene, and then go over what's left of the two planes to see what you can determine about possible malfunctions. Then I want you to return home and write a report that exonerates our plane and confirms the Air Force's conclusion that the cause was pilot error.

"While you are at it, check out the previous incidents and interview the pilots who didn't crash. I want to be sure that we leave no stone unturned in our investigation to prove that our airplane is completely safe. Is everything clear?" Mr. Stern ended with a severe look for a few seconds and then broke into a big smile. "I know you'll do a great job and look forward to reading your report."

Mr. Stern rose and held out his hand as the signal that the meeting was over. "And by the way, I've instructed all departments to give you any help you need. Just ask."

Steve nodded, rose out of his chair, shook hands, smiled, thanked his boss again and tuned to walk out of the conference room. "Also, I'd like your report in two weeks." Steve turned back and nodded as he walked out quickly before he received any more directions.

CHAPTER THREE

Steve sat with his head back and his feet on the corner of the desk. He looked around the room at the pictures on the wall. They were photos of the various fighter planes the company had built during and after World War II. He thought back over the ones he had flown in combat. His eyes closed as he thought about how well most were designed and how difficult others had been to fly.

He was sitting in the office of the company's Chief of Product Design, an old friend of his from the war. Ben Crawford was a talented engineer and a good manager of men, not necessarily compatible qualities as Steve had come to learn over the years. Steve admired him for both skills.

The door suddenly opened and a tall slim man with slightly graying hair walked in with his head staring down at the floor. "Hi Ben!" Steve said with a smile as he moved his feet off of Ben's desk.

Ben looked up with a startled expression. "Well hello Steve. To what do I owe this pleasant surprise?" He continued over to his desk chair, settled in, and leaned back to match Steve's relaxed position. "Can I get you a cup of coffee?"

"No, Ben thanks. Actually I dropped by to talk business."

"Yes, I've been expecting you. Mr. Stern recently told me that he was bringing you in on our F-87 problem." Ben reached in his desk and brought out a pack of cigarettes and lit one up. "Care for a smoke Steve?" Ben slid the pack across the desk.

"No thanks. I want to pick your brain on this problem that's causing so much stir in Washington and here in LA." Ben squirmed in his chair, rotating it to look out the window while blowing smoke rings toward the ceiling, listening to Steve.

"This is my first encounter with the Leopard as you call it. So I don't know quite where to begin. I've read some newspaper reports that don't sound good. Can you give me a background so I will know where to begin?

"Okay." Ben turned back to face him. "There's a problem with the Leopard that is causing it to fall out of the sky, but no one seems to know why. Pilots have been killed, and those that survived have told us that the plane suddenly lunges sideways, sometimes on landing approach and sometimes shortly after takeoff. If it happens close to the ground, the pilot typically can't regain control before it hits the ground. Inspections of the crash site have so far shown that all of the fight controls are in the proper position: ailerons, flaps, elevators and rudder surfaces are where they should be. As a consequence, the Air Force has ruled all of the crashes as 'pilot error', which makes the guys who fly the Leopard very angry. They say that the pilots of these downed planes are far too skilled to have caused these crashes." Ben turned away again and seemed to be lost in thought.

Steve paused for a minute and then continued. "And you designers have no idea what might be causing this problem?"

Ben turned toward him again. "Not the slightest idea, Steve. We've all gone over the design time and time again and have found nothing. You might think that it was sabotage, but that can't be that either. You and I have worked together for many years, and I have never seen anything like this. Skilled, experienced pilots are loosing control of their planes and nosing over into the ground, ending in a ball of fire and exploding metal. And this is a plane whose design I supervised." His voice trailed off.

Steve could tell that this was all he was going to get from Ben this day. He stood and headed for the door. "I think I'll head up to McChord to take a look at the latest to crash and see what I can find."

"Good luck Steve." Ben was still staring out the window as Steve closed the office door behind him.

Steve walked to his car in the parking lot and slid into the driver's seat. He was happy to be going home before the rush hour traffic hit the roads. He drove out of the large parking lot onto Hawthorne Boulevard and headed south toward his home in Palos Verdes.

"Boy will I be glad when they build more freeways around here," he thought as he began to hit stoplights. Stoplights always bothered him. He thought that it was God telling him that he needed to go to church more often. But his wife always said, "Relax and spend a red light meditating on how lucky we are."

There were lots of red lights in Los Angeles, he thought. The trip soon turned into a blur as his mind wandered off into his new assignment. He thought about his talk with his old friend Ben. There had been something strange about his body language that Steve was usually good at reading. However, he couldn't pinpoint what was bothering him about Ben's that day.

He finally turned into his driveway and parked next to his wife's new Buick sitting on her side of the garage. He got out of his Ford and looked out to his favorite view, the Pacific Ocean. Their home was not one of the elite upper crust homes on the peninsula, but it was the best home they had ever had. He had just barely been able to afford it last year when he and his wife had mortgaged everything they had to be able to move in. "You know you will soon get a raise, Honey, and this kind of a home won't come on the market again soon." He knew that his wife and their realtor had conspired against him, but he loved their new home too.

He walked up the long walkway and turned again to look out over the Pacific with the afternoon sun glimmering off the distant waves. "Maybe she was right," he thought as he turned the key and walked into the big entry hall. "Hi Honey. I'm home!"

Ellen was working in their back yard, pruning rose bushes in preparation for the soon-to-be-arriving spring-time. She was a very attractive, not-quit-middle-aged woman with her blond hair curled and pulled back. Steve liked her hair better when they were married. Ellen had worn it longer, with loose waves hanging around her shoulders. Still, she looked much younger than she actually was. When she heard Steve's voice, she jumped up, and tossed a stray strand out of her face, and came running into the house to greet her husband.

She threw her arms around him and gave him a big kiss. "Hi, Sweetheart. What are you doing home so early?" Steve gave her a big hug and took off his coat.

"I have to go on a trip tomorrow, so they let me come home early"

"Oh dear. Where are you going? You remember that we have a bridge date with the Sommers on Friday. I do hope that you will be home on time. It's important that we don't stand them up. They are the most important family here in our neighborhood."

Steve enjoyed playing bridge with his wife. She was good, almost a good a player as he, and he particularly liked beating the Sommers. They had only played together once before, but he and Ellen had beat them badly. "I will do my best, but can't guarantee anything."

Ellen, wearing shorts, sat down in her chair in the living room. Steve couldn't help but admire her beautiful legs that were now crossed. "So tell me where are you going this time."

Steve stretched out on the sofa and undid his tie. "I'm flying up to Seattle in the morning, where I'll be picked up by an adjutant who will drive me south to McChord Air Force base in Tacoma. I have an appointment with the base commander to talk about the recent crashes of our new jet fighter, the Leopard. The boss has just given me the assignment to find out what's been causing them to crash."

"Yes, I have been reading about that. Mr. Stern must really think a lot of you to give you such an assignment." She smiled at him with a smile that made her face light up as the light coming through the window made her hair shine.

"And oh, by the way, Mr. Stern presented me with an award plaque today in front of all the department heads for the work I did on solving the metal fatigue failure problem."

Now Ellen jumped up, ran over and knelt down next to him on the floor. She let her hair fall down on his face as he loved her to do and gave him a big kiss. "Someday you will have his job. You are the best test engineer they've got." She turned her head and laid it down on his chest. He reached down and ran his hands through her hair and kissed the top of her head.

14

"Okay, what are you two up to," they heard as the door slammed behind their thirteen year old daughter, Jennifer. She had blond hair and blue eyes like her mother but still moved with the gawkiness of a young teenager rather than with her mother's athletic ease.

"Oh dear. School must be out." Steve answered. The two unlocked their embrace and rose off the sofa to greet her. After hugs all around, she added, "I'd love to stay and chat, but I need to call Susan," as she tossed her books on the table and skipped off into her bedroom.

"Wait a minute. Didn't she just ride home with her friend Susan on the school bus?" Steve looked startled.

"Yes dear. But they always get together on the phone afterward to talk about what went on at school today and what the boys are doing. You don't remember that part of growing up because you were never a girl. At least its better than watching television." Ellen smiled at him as she walked toward the kitchen. "Now its time to start dinner."

"And oh by the way, I also got a raise today," he said as she disappeared into the kitchen.

"Yes dear. I know. We'll decide what to do with it after dinner." She had just stuck her head back into the living room with that mischievous grin on her face.

"Maybe we can now make the payments on this house," Steve said. Ellen chuckled but didn't respond.

Later that evening, Steve and Ellen sat next to their pool enjoying a cup of coffee and watching the sunset over the ocean. Matt 15, had come home from baseball practice, and Carolyn 11, had returned from her friend's house. Now all three kids were doing homework in their rooms, and the dog was curled up on the patio sleeping. "My goodness you are quiet tonight," Ellen looked over at him.

"There is something I don't get about this whole thing. Mr. Stern said that he is anxiously awaiting my report confirming that the problems were all pilot error. It was obvious that he is concerned more about what our customer thinks than trying to find and fix a problem with our new plane. And then there's Ben. His body language was disturbing although I can't say why exactly. If no one else has found a problem with the plane, why would I do any better? I'm going to look at the wreckage of two planes that will be nothing more than a pile of burned aluminum. Then I'll write a report that the crash was indeed 'pilot error' and go back to work, while other planes fall out of the sky and young men are killed. Do they really believe that these were all pilot error crashes or are they hiding something?"

I'm sure that if the president of your company wants your report to support the Air Force, you will figure out a way to accommodate him." Ellen put her head on his shoulder. Steve didn't respond.

CHAPTER FOUR

The airliner dropped into the clouds as Steve was admiring the soaring peak of Mount Rainer jutting into the sky to his right before it disappeared from view. The plane began to shutter as the wheels came down and the wind caught the additional drag, causing the plane to roll slightly around its longitudinal axis. "This must be what the pilots felt when their planes lost control," he mumbled to himself.

He always disliked this part of the trip, when the airliner dropped into the clouds lying just a few thousand feet above the ground. He knew that they would soon break beneath the layer, where the pilot could see again. But in the meantime they were all at the mercy of the ground controller who, everyone hoped, was watching their plane on radar and talking to the pilot, and not out on a coffee break.

Walking out of the baggage claim area with his suitcase hanging from the strap draped over his shoulder, he saw what he was looking for, an Air Force officer holding up a sign with the name Mr. Pritchard on it. He walked up, set his bag down and introduced himself with a big handshake. "Hi Major, my name is Steve."

"Good morning Mr. Pritchard, my mane is Major Pat

Hoskins, and I'm your chauffer today." The major spoke with a bit more formality than the occasion required but had a big grin, so Steve thought that he was probably an okay person.

"Our car is waiting for us in the hourly parking zone. It shouldn't take long to get to McChord now that the commute traffic has died down."

Steve watched the houses pass by as they headed south toward Tacoma. "So what is the story on these fighters going down for no apparent reason?"

"Well Mr. Pritchard, I can't tell you too much for two reasons. One is that I don't know much, but the other is that the colonel wants to brief you himself. All I can say is that it is a serious problem either of pilot training or of some structural or other defect in the design of your fighter plane. So far, the consensus seems to be that the pilots have not learned how to fly the F-87 yet, and some are dying because of it. The pilots don't agree with that of course, but there seems to be no other conclusion since we can find nothing wrong with the planes at the crash scene. I guess that's what you're here for." The major turned and smiled weakly at Steve who nodded.

They slowed to take a salute from an MP as they drove through the gate and then turned toward the administration building. They pulled up into a parking place near the main entrance with the major's name on it. "I suspect that the colonel's waiting for you."

"Hi Margaret. Let me introduce Mr. Pritchard from Western Aircraft to see the colonel." The staff sergeant smiled and mumbled something, and Steve responded politely. "Would you please tell the colonel that Mr. Pritchard is here?"

"Sure Major. Why don't you two sit over there while I tell him." She rose, pointing to two chairs against the wall, and walked into the colonel's office, shutting the door behind her. She soon returned with the colonel following her.

"Good morning Mr. Pritchard. May I call you Steve?"

Steve replied, "Of course, Colonel," shook his hand and they exchanged pleasantries.

"Please come into my office. There are a number of things I want to share with you before you start your investigation." The colonel ushered Steve into his office and shut the door behind them.

Steve couldn't help but look at the many photos hanging along the walls, especially the big painting behind his desk. "I guess you were a P-38 pilot during the war," Steve finally said admiring the painting of a Lightning firing at a Zero going down in flames over Guadalcanal. "Wow, that's quite a painting. That isn't you in that plane is it?"

"No, actually that painting was made by a friend of mine and presented it to me on my fifth kill. I do miss those days. But as I'm sure you know, the P-38 was not appropriate for use in Northern Europe, especially during the winter, so they sent us to the Pacific," he said as he motioned Steve to sit down across from him. "I could never figure out why Lockheed engineers couldn't design a heater system that would keep the cockpit warm, especially when we were flying over 30,000 feet. Man it was colder than a witches elbow up there. When the P-47's and the P-51's arrived, they shipped us over to the South Pacific where it was warmer, and we wouldn't freeze to death. Would you like a cup of coffee?"

"No thank you Colonel. I had a couple on the plane."

"I understand you got a few of those Krauts yourself and are still a major in the reserve. Have you flown any of the new jets that you guys are building?"

"I have flown several times in Lockheed's F-80's, but haven't tried our new F-87 Leopard yet. I hear that they actually break the sound barrier and are lots of fun to fly, unless they don't stay up where they belong." The colonel offered a bit of a smile in response.

"Actually, I think I broke the sound barrier in a P-38 once in the spring of 1945 over the Philippines." The colonel leaned back in his chair and stared out his window. "There were no more Japs to shoot down, so we were trying to find something to do to keep amused. I took my plane up to 40,000 feet, pointed the nose downward and shoved the throttles all the way forward. Boy it was a screaming ride down. The speedometer pinned out at 500 miles per hour and the plane shuttered as I approached the ground. I really believe that I did break Mach One, but no one back in the States would believe me."

"You were really lucky that the P-38 didn't come apart at that speed. You must have been flying one of the "J" models with the dive break under the wings because, as you know, the compressibility shock wave kicked in at 500 MPH and often disintegrated the tail assembly. Few pilots lived to tell about it," Steve responded.

Steve couldn't resist himself. "There were several P-38 pilots and the Air Force itself who have claimed the same thing Colonel. But it was actually impossible for any World War II aircraft to break the sound barrier. The German jets came the closest and of course the V-2 did it all the time." He was watching the expression on the colonel's face. "The main problem was that the Mach indictor had not been invented yet, and our wing designs created such shock waves over the top of the wings that exceeding Mach One was not possible until Colonel Yeager did it in 1947. As you know, the speed of sound increase as you get closer to the ground, so at the same speed, your Mach number actually decreases in a dive as the air density increases." Steve ended with a smile. He thought it better too give the colonel a little wiggle room.

"Yes. Well, we are not here to rehash World Was II are we? I need to bring you up to date on the crashes we have been having in your company's F-87. Actually, not all have happened here at McChord, but we've the newest squadron of them, so we've had our share. As you know it is our prime defense against the Soviet's big four-engine bomber, the TU-95 that we call the Bear. Our squadron of Leopards here at McChord is our first line of defense against any attack by them coming down from Siberia.

"Let me generalize a bit because there is a disturbing similarity in all of the accidents that I have seen and read about. First of all, they have happened at low altitude, either on takeoff or landing, or when the plane is approaching stalling speed. The plane suddenly spins out of control, sometimes to the right and sometimes to the left. And of course as you know, being close to the ground spells trouble. The pilots have little time to correct the problem before the plane hits the ground. However, not all planes have crashed. Several pilots have regained control and landed their planes safely. In all cases, inspections have revealed no flight surface out of position. It's almost as if a giant, invisible hand, has reached out of the sky, grabbed the plane, twisted it and then let go. It's scary." The colonel watched the expression on Steve's face.

"I agree with you Colonel. There's no known reason that this could have happened, but obviously it has. So I need to find the cause. At least that's what I get paid to do, so where do I begin?"

"I suggest that you first of all travel out to the site of the latest crash and see what you can find. Two F-87 interceptors scrambled on a training flight to intercept fictitious incoming enemy bombers flying down from Siberia. The flight leader was an experienced pilot, a first lieutenant, and his wingman was also quite familiar with his job. Unfortunately the wingman accelerated a bit faster than normal, so when they lifted off the runway he was to the right and almost even with his leader. This in itself was a pilot error.

"They poured on the coal and were airborne rapidly. At an altitude of a couple of hundred feet, the wingman suddenly turned sharply to his left and collided with the flight leader. The two planes fell to the ground and burst into flames killing both pilots instantly. Our investigation revealed nothing out of the ordinary in either plane, so we ruled it pilot error. Maybe you can find something we overlooked."

"I'll certainly try Colonel." Steve rose from his chair, turned and walked to the door.

"Major Hoskins will take you wherever you want to go, and if you need anything, let me know."

"Yes sir."

"Oh wait! I almost forgot. The Air Force brass has hired an independent consultant, an expert in airfoil design, to help you in your search. I believe that Dr. Charlie Collins is scheduled to meet you at the crash site today. That's all." The colonel sat back down at his desk and picked up the phone.

Just what I need, an "independent consultant" looking over my shoulder, Steve thought to himself with some sarcasm as he walked out of the building.

CHAPTER FIVE

Steve picked carefully through the remnants of what once had been two F-87 fighter jets. They had been piled up without much regard for access to their remaining parts. "It is almost as if they don't want me to find anything," Steve thought. He pulled out sheets of aluminum and tossed them aside, trying to avoid letting the sharp edges cut his hands. It suddenly occurred to him that he should have brought gloves.

He looked up in time to see an Air Force car driving toward him. "Great. Now I get to meet Charlie or whatever his name is. He'll probably want me to call him Doctor," Steve mumbled. He turned and went back to work rummaging through the wreckage. He heard the car door slam and footsteps headed toward him. He was studying a particular piece of a wing when a voice interrupted his thoughts. "The aileron you are looking at is in the down position, because the pilot was probably trying to correct for the roll before he lost complete control of his plane."

Steve dropped the wing section and looked up in disbelief. She was standing about ten feet away in the midst of engine parts looking at him with a slight smile. She was dressed in slacks and tennis shoes and wearing a bulky sweater. As he looked at her face, he saw an attractive, but not beautiful, young woman with light brown hair tied behind her head looking at him with intense brown eyes. He estimated that she was in her mid twenties. He opened his mouth but nothing came out.

"But let me introduce myself. I am Dr. Charlie Collins, a graduated in aeronautical engineering from Stanford, and hired by the Air Force to help you identify the reason why these planes have been crashing. You must be Steve Pritchard." Charlie glanced over his 5ft. 10-inch frame with its broad shoulders with lots of dark brown hair streaked with grey. She estimated him to be in his early forties.

"Yes I am," was all Steve could think to reply. As he finished, his foot slipped off a piece of aluminum and he caught himself just before he lost balance. "I—I---I---"

"You were expecting a man by the name of Charlie. Yes, I know. They all say that. My real name is Charlene, but I prefer Charlie, and that's what you may call me."

Having finally recovered from his initial shock, Steve mumbled, "Okay Charlie, let's get to work." He lifted up the wing section. tipped it toward her and asked, "How did you know that this aileron was not the cause of the plane's rotation and the accident?"

She took several steps toward him and pointed at the piece in his hand. "In the first place, notice that it is a left, not the right wing. In the second place, by looking at the fuselage to which it was attached, you can see that this was the plane that rotated into the flight leader and caused the collision. Its nose was completed destroyed when they collided. Also, eyewitness accounts of the accident all say that the wingman was on the right side of the two-plane formation as is Air Force custom. Therefore, he rotated to his left, which is the opposite direction that the aileron position is now. Obviously, the wingman was frantically trying to stop the left rotation by forcing the plane to rotate back to the right. Unfortunately, he could not correct the left hand rotation in time, so he collided with the flight leader. I suspect that if we look into the cockpit, we will see the control stick jammed hard to the right."

Steve followed her finger back and forth during her conversation and looked at her quizzically. Without saying anything, he walked over to what was left of the cockpit and looked into it. He turned back toward her. "You're right, but I didn't doubt you for a minute."

"Wait a minute." He stared back into the cockpit. "The Air Force has concluded that this accident was caused by pilot error. If the wingman had initiated a turn too soon, as that conclusion implies, this aileron would be in the up position, and the stick would be jammed in the left turn position. But as you say the opposite is true."

"Very good Steve. May I call you Steve?" She walked over to the cockpit without waiting for an answer. "So what exactly are we looking for," she asked as she peered into the cockpit?

"Well I am trying to identify the cause of this wreck. I can't say what you're looking for exactly." He regretted his comment as soon as he made it and turned back toward the wreckage. She was quiet for a while, following him as he walked through the wreckage searching for clues.

Then, Charlie stopped and put her hands on her hips. "So I guess we have to have this out before we go any further. I am not here because I asked for this job. My boss sent me here at the request of General Adams, the head of procurement for the Air Force in Washington, D.C. When a four star general asks for something, you respond, right? The Air Force has as big an interest in this airplane as does your company. In fact I would say that it is bigger because they're paying the bill, and, they're also given the responsibility of protecting this country.

"I know that you, the big World War II ace, don't like someone following you around, and you probably hate it more because I am a woman. However, that is my job, and I hope that we can learn to get along. It will make both of our tasks easier." She stood staring at him.

"Well, you made your point, --- I need to straighten out my attitude I guess," Steve finally responded. "Yes, you're right. I was a hero once. At least that's what everyone called me." Steve sat down on a piece of wreckage. "There are twelve German pilots who probably wouldn't agree with you on that however. A few bailed out and are probably still alive, cursing my name. However, that war is over, and now let's win this one.

"Let's start over." He reached out his hand. "Hi, My name is Steve and you must be Charlie." He stood up with a big grin on his face. She let out a little sigh, shook his hand but said nothing. They both continued looking though the wreckage, tossing burnt and twisted pieces of aluminum aside as they walked and sometimes crawled through what was left of the two planes.

CHAPTER SIX

"Well that was a wasted day." Steve sipped his gin and tonic and stared into the nearby fireplace. Charlie set down her glass of wine and looked back at him.

"Oh, I don't know. We're now able to show that the crash wasn't caused by the wingman turning too soon into the flight leader. It's strange that the Air Force would conclude that pilot error was the cause when they not only had no proof of that, but there was actually proof that it was not."

"My assumption is that, since they could find no mechanical problem or control surface position that would have caused the rotation, they had to come up with some reason. And pilot error was all that was left." Steve said as he watched the flames dancing in the fireplace.

"I didn't know that you were still in the reserve. Steve. It's great that you could get us into this officers' club. I doubt there's as good a bar for miles around." She took another sip of her wine.

"Nor as cheap," Steve smiled as he raised his glass in salute to her.

"So what are you going to do now?" Charlie joined Steve in staring at the dancing flames in the fireplace.

"Well there is a pilot here on the base who has experienced this rotation problem but was able to get control before the plane crashed and he has survived." Charlie turned away from the fire to look at him.

"I've asked the colonel to have him meet us here and relate his experience to us." Steve looked at his watch. "In fact, he should be here at any minute."

After a few minutes of silence, the front door to the officers' club opened and in walked a young first lieutenant who removed his hat and looked around the bar. Steve stood up and waved to the officer. As the lieutenant approached their table, Steve reached out and shook his hand and introduced himself and Charlie. The lieutenant smiled and replied, "I'm Lieutenant Mel Jacobson, and I understand you are investigating the recent crashes of the F-87."

"Yes. In fact we both are," as Steve waved toward Charlie. She couldn't help but be amazed at how much his attitude had changed since this afternoon. Steve motioned to the lieutenant to join them. "What can we get you to drink?" They both sat down as the lieutenant responded, "I'll have a beer, thank you, Sir." Steve motioned for the waiter to come over.

"So, Lieutenant, the colonel tells me that you are one of the few pilots who has survived this mysterious malfunction, on the F-87."

"Please, Sir, call me Mel, and yes I did land safely after being thrown around a bit in the midst of landing. It was scary to say the least."

"Okay, Mel. Tell us what happened." Steve opened his notebook ready to write.

"Well, Sir, I was coming in for a landing here at McChord a couple of weeks ago in my F-87, and everything went fine on the downwind leg. I turned for the final approach, dropped my airspeed and got ready to deploy my flaps. As I approached stall speed, and before I could react, my plane suddenly twisted to the right. It wasn't exactly a turn, just a rotation about the longitudinal axis. I immediately jammed my stick hard to the left to counteract the roll. My reaction worked, the rotation stopped after about ninety degrees, and the plane returned to an upright position. In fact, I had over corrected a bit and the plane went into a left rotation. However, I had control by then and was able to bring it back to a horizontal position. The plane responded as it should, and I was able to get down successfully. I walked around and inspected the wings and tail surfaces after securing the engine and could find nothing out of the ordinary. That's about it."

"Hmmm. Charlie, do you have any questions? Steve was writing in his notebook.

"The key here is that it was not a turn, but a rotation. That seems to rule out a problem with the rudder control surfaces," Charlie seemed to ask and say in one sentence. Mel nodded as no one could think of anything else to say.

"We need to remember that the F-87 did have problems with their flaps when it was first built. When the pilot deployed the flaps, they would not deploy evenly, and the pilots would loss control for a few seconds. But that problem was solved some time ago, and besides, the flaps are so close to the fuselage that their uneven deployment would not cause such a violent reaction. The only other control surfaces on the wings are the ailerons, and they are controlled together. Unfortunately, I still don't have a good explanation for what happened," Steve said as he could think of no additional questions.

"Also, I hadn't yet reached to the flaps lever when the rotation started," Mel added.

"Yes, I almost forgot," Charlie added.

"Well thank you Mel. If you can think of anything you

have forgotten, please call me." Steve gave him his card.

"I will Sir." Mel finished his beer and stood up to leave. "I have to say that I am reluctant to fly that plane again until somebody can identify the problem."

"Yes, Mel, we understand and are working as hard as we can." Steve stood up, smiled and shook Mel's hand. "Maybe we will see you again soon." Mel walked out the door.

"So what have we learned that we didn't know?

"Not much," Steve responded. "Let's have dinner and call it a day. I have to meet with the colonel tomorrow, but let's take one last look at a F-87 in the hanger in the morning. I'll meet you there at 0900."

CHAPTER SEVEN

Steve stood staring at the wing of the F-87 sitting in the hanger. "It must be the wing," he thought. "But what part of the wing?" He walked up to the plane and rubbed his hands along the fuselage and then the wing. "Can I help you sir? Steve turned around to see a master sergeant walking toward him.

"Good morning Sergeant. Well I don't know. I'm trying to figure out what is causing these planes to go down without any apparent cause. My name is Steve Pritchard"

"Yes I know Sir. My name is Sergeant Jacobs. I'm in charge of the ground crews that work on these planes. I would be happy to answer any questions you might have." Before Steve could ask him how he knew his name, the door to the hanger opened, and Charlie walked in.

"Well good morning Charlie. Did you get a good night's sleep? By the way, let me introduce you to the ground crew chief here, Master Sergeant Jacobs. He was just offering me help in solving our problem. Maybe he has some answers for us." He turned back to the airplane as Charlie walked up to them.

"I'm glad to meet you Sergeant," Charlie said. Turning back to Steve she continued, " I've nothing to add to our dilemma. I'm as baffled as you are. I tossed and turned all night trying to put everything together and have come up with nothing." The sergeant stood silently as he watched the two walking around the plane.

Steve finally looked over at him. "Sergeant. I would like to take this plane up for a short spin. Do you think you could arrange that for me?"

"Yes, Sir. Give me an hour or so, and I'll have it ready for take off."

"Great Sergeant. I will be back in an hour." He took Charlie by the arm, and the two of them walked out of the hanger.

"Are you sure you should be taking this plane up? You have never flown one before, and they do have a habit of crashing." She stopped walking and looked up at him. Steve smiled and looked up at the sky.

"I've flown almost everything the Air Force has and I don't think this one will be a problem. Besides I don't intend to break the sound barrier or do any fancy maneuvers. I just want to get its feel and see how it behaves around stall speeds. That seems to be where the problems have occurred."

The two of them walked out to the flight line toward the jet now warming up with its soft whine. Steve put on his flight helmet and climbed up toward the cockpit. He tried not to show his nervousness.

Sergeant Jacobs was standing on the wing to help Steve into the cockpit. As he strapped himself in, Sergeant Jacobs pointed out the controls to Steve, "This model has a cockpit that rotates backward when you push this handle, so you can evacuate quickly in an emergency." Steve could barely hear him over the noise of the engine warming up. He nevertheless nodded his understanding. He was happy that the new jet fighters all had tricycle landing gears instead of the tail draggers that was common on all of the World War II fighters except the P-38 and P-39. He could actually see over the nose.

Charlie was standing a short distance away watching intently. Sergeant Jacobs jumped down from the wing, and Steve closed the canopy. He studied the instrument panel intently for a couple of minutes to familiarize himself with the controls. The instrument cluster was slightly different than the ones he had used.

Two ground crewmen finally removed the blocks from the tires, and Steve slowly pushed the throttle forward as the F-87 moved out across the taxiway and turned toward the runway.

Although he had flown jets a couple of times, he was still use to the rattle and vibration of the piston engine in which he had become an ace during the war. And the smell was different. There was no odor of overly rich exhaust swirling around the cockpit. "The noise of a turbo jet was certainly different from that of the old Pratt and Whitneys," he thought.

He turned onto the runway heading upwind, set the brakes and accelerated the engine listening for any malfunction. There was none, at least that he could hear. He was always amazed at how smooth the jets were. He throttled down and released the brakes. There was still enough thrust to cause the plane to jump ahead like a jackrabbit. He rapidly picked up speed along the runway.

As he accelerated, he pulled back on the stick and lifted off smartly. "Boy this thing has got some soup," he thought. When he was sure that he was clear of the runway, he reached down, raised the landing gear and then pushed the flaps lever into its stowed position.

He watched the airspeed intently as it passed one fifty and approached two hundred knots. He felt the vibration and then the reaction of the stick in his hand and peddles under his feet as he anticipated some kind of a malfunction. But nothing unusual happened. "Boy I sure do miss flying," he said to himself.

There were only light winds and scattered clouds that day, so as his altitude and airspeed increased, he turned slightly to his right so that he could have a good view of the Olympic Range on his left and Mount Rainier on his right. Ahead he could see the beautiful harbor of Seattle with ferryboats crossing the bay. "Boy this is a beautiful place to live, but I'm not up here to sightsee," he thought, as he began a slow turn to his left to keep away from the landing approach to the Seattle airport.

He turned sharply to the right and then to the left, and then put it into a barrel roll and then a sudden dive to see how the plane responded. It performed beautifully. He jammed the throttle forward and then back to see if the engine flamed out, but again nothing happened. He deployed the flaps to be sure that they deployed evenly and they did. Again, he felt nothing unusual.

After several minutes of trying everything he could think of, he turned and headed back toward the runway on his downwind approach. After getting permission to land from the air flight controller, he turned into his final approach upwind. This would be the acid test. "Many of the accidents had happened in the final approach," he thought.

He slowed to stall speed, dropped his flaps and then the landing gear. The plane kept a steady course. He landed a bit hard with the nose up slightly hoping to cause a problem to show itself. The landing was perfect, although a little rough. He slowed and taxied over to the hanger, turned into the plane's parking place and shut off the engine. He opened the cockpit canopy and took off his helmet.

"Welcome back." Charlie came running up to the plane

as he jumped onto the tarmac. "Did you have any problems? It looked good from down here," she said. Sergeant Jacobs came walking up from the hanger with a smile of relief on his face.

"Everything went fine. I saw no problems anywhere, so now I'm as confused as ever." Steve put his arm around her shoulder as they headed toward the hanger.

This was not so much a show of affection as it was an acceptance that she was one of the guys. "Let's have some lunch and plan our presentation for the colonel this afternoon."

"So what are you going to say to the colonel this afternoon?" Charlie was finishing up her chicken salad.

Steve set down his almost empty glass of beer and took the last bite out of his roast beef sandwich. He shook his head. "Hell if I know!

"Obviously I have to be honest, don't you think? I mean what have we discovered that would discount pilot error? Yet the fact that it has happened so consistently disproves pilot error by definition. The loss of control all happened at low altitude to experienced pilots, and those who survived all said that they did nothing to cause the problem. My boss has sure given me a tough first assignment," Steve said as he drained his glass.

Charlie smiled at him and finally said, "Actually its your second assignment, but who's counting?" She then turned her gaze out the window where she could see the F-87's parked in front of the hanger. "You know Steve that I don't know much about airplane design except what they taught me at Stanford. But there was something strange that I remember seeing at the crash site that we haven't talked about."

Steve looked quizzically at her as he finished up his sandwich. "What's that?"

"Well, when you were studying the flaps on the wing of the wingman's plane, you buried the forward part of the wing in the ground. And when you stopped looking at it, you dropped it back down under the fuselage and probably didn't notice it."

"Didn't notice what?"

"I don't know what to call it exactly. It ran along the forward edge of the wing almost its entire length and looked to be about eight or so inches in depth. It looked a little like a wing flap, but it was on the leading edge of the wing and was not extended. It looked to be a part of the wing, whatever it was, and that's about all I can say about it." Charlie folded her hands on her lap and stared at Steve.

"Why didn't you call it to my attention?"

"I thought you saw it. You were right on top of it."

"Hmmm. I must have had my mind on something else. I just don't remember seeing it. Before we meet the colonel let's go back to the hanger and take a look.

"That's a good idea, but it just occurred to me that the plane you flew didn't have that thing, whatever it is, on it. I just remembered."

Steve got up from the table and stared at her. "Let's go back to the hanger now."

They walked through the door and saw Steve's plane sitting in the center of the hanger. Steve grabbed Charlie's arm and stopped. "Look. My plane is sitting right in the center where I would be sure to see it. I wonder if that is by design?" They continued walking toward it.

"Our friendly master sergeant is not around. He must be still out to lunch." Charlie searched around the hanger as Steve walked up to the plane.

Steve ran his hand along the forward edge of the wing. "There's nothing here like you described."

"That's true mister smart guy! Remember that's what I

told you back at the club." She had her arms folded across her chest.

Steve grinned but didn't respond as he stood back from the plane to survey the rest of the hanger. "This is the only F-87 in the hanger. There must be others around. Let's go through the side door over there and see what we can find."

They walked briskly out the door and found themselves in a second hanger. "We didn't see these." They stared around at a half dozen or so F-87's in various stages of repair, but no one was working on them. "These guys must be out to lunch too. The Air Force sure takes long lunch breaks; we didn't get to do that during the war." Charlie walked away from Steve toward the nearest plane that appeared to be having an engine overhaul. "Come over here Steve and take a look at this."

Steve let out a small gasp as he saw what appeared to be extended wing flaps along the leading edge of both wings. He rubbed his hand along the front edge and said, "These have the same contour as the forward part of the wing but are extended out about six or eight inches for some reason."

Charlie added, "It seems to give the wing more area."

"Well, no telling where I'll find you two!"

Steve and Charlie spun around and saw Master Sergeant Jacobs walking briskly toward them across the floor. "Yea, no telling," Steve managed a response. "So tell us Sergeant. What is this thing here?" Steve ran his hand along the extended forward edge of the wing.

"Those are called slats, Sir."

"Whenever the sergeant said sir, it lent a bit of sarcasm to the word," Steve thought. "They are intended to add a little more lift when the plane is taking off or landing. That's about all I know about them, Sir" His comment cut off what appeared to be another question forming in

Steve's mind.

"So why didn't the plane Steve flew this morning have them?" Charlie's voice sounded a bit more determined than she intended.

The sergeant smiled. "The one Mr. Pritchard flew is brand new and just arrived a few days ago. I thought he would enjoy flying the latest model." The sergeant's expression indicated that that was about all he was going to say on the subject. "We cannot permit anyone to be around these planes while they are being repaired. Safety and security reasons you know." The sergeant waved for them to follow him out of the hanger.

"It's time to go see the colonel, Charlie. We don't want to keep him waiting." Steve took her arm and directed her toward the main offices as they left the hanger buildings.

"So what's up with that guy?" Charlie, with her shorter legs, was trying frantically to keep up with Steve's long strides.

They walked into the colonel's outer office. "Oh there you are." The colonel's secretary looked up from her desk. "I have been looking for you to tell you that the colonel has to cancel his meeting with you this afternoon. He has been called to a meeting at headquarters in Seattle. He apologizes, Mr. Pritchard, and says to tell you that he looks forward to reading your report." She smiled and folded her hands on her desk. Steve looked over at Charlie.

"Well I guess that's it for us. Let's get to the airport and head home." Charlie nodded and picked up her briefcase. They walked into the waiting sedan into which someone had put their luggage, got in and headed toward the SeaTac Airport.

CHAPTER EIGHT

"I've got to check on those slats. After all my years of flying and designing aircraft, I've never heard of them. I'm thinking that there are several people in LA who can help me." Steve was sipping on his beer waiting for his plane to board. Charlie didn't respond. She, too, was trying to figure out what she had seen.

"I have some searching to do too. There are a few people at Ames who might help us. Let's keep in touch; there is the old 'two heads are better than one' issue here." She smiled at Steve through her glass of chardonnay. Steve returned her smile but he didn't think she would have much to offer.

"Well at least, it will be good to get home," he said.

"Maybe good for you. But I am back living with my parents in Santa Clara Valley and trying to build a life after my husband pulled up stakes and left a few months ago. He couldn't put up with a wife who had a PhD in aeronautical engineering. Men can still be strange about their wives making more money than they do. But I guess I'm really lucky to have parents to fall back on." She set her glass down and looked sadly out the window at the airliners taking off.

Steve looked at her for a few minutes. "I'm sorry. I didn't know. I guess that home means different things to each of us doesn't it?"

Charlie turned back toward him. "No problems mate, as our Australian friends would say." She was smiling again. "You must solve this problem, and I'll do whatever I can to help you. We have each other's phone numbers, so let's use them if we find anything." They raised their glasses and nodded to each other.

A loud speaker announced the boarding of the flight to San Jose, so Charlie stood and sipped the last of her wine. She picked up her suitcase in one hand, her briefcase in the other, and nodded at Steve saying, "Keep in touch." She put the briefcase strap over one shoulder waved with her now empty hand, turned and walked toward the boarding area. She figured that she would probably never hear from him again.

Steve watched her walk away noticing her figure for the first time. He was not good at colors, but it seemed that her well fitted, modestly short beige skirt and light brown blouse accented her hair very well. He liked the way she walked, the way she carried herself, with confidence but not arrogance. He watched her until she disappeared into the boarding section then turned back to his beer, wondering if he would see her again. He didn't know that she was looking up into a pane of glass that reflected Steve sitting back at his table watching her. She smiled slightly to herself.

His plane was called in a little while. Climbing aboard with everyone else, he slumped into his seat and immediately closed his eyes. "Now for a little nap," he mumbled as he fell asleep before they left the ground.

They hit the runway with a jolt at LA International as he rubbed the sleep out of his eyes. I've got to talk with the guys who designed the F-87 and figure out what's going on, he thought. He walked out of the baggage claim area to his car carrying his suitcase and slid into the driver's seat. He drove out onto Sepulveda and headed south to the plant.

Steve parked in the one place left, walked to the engineering design building and headed up to the main office. He saw the sign, Chief Engineer, and opened the door. Ben's secretary was typing frantically but stopped to look up. "Oh hi, Steve. Ben is in. Let me announce you." She turned to her intercom system and pushed the button. "Ben, Steve is here to see you." She turned back. "He says to come on in. He has been expecting you." She went back to her typing.

"Steve. It's good to see you. Sit! Can I get you a coffee?"

"No thanks Ben. I had a couple on the flight down."

"Okay, so how was your trip?" Ben leaned back in his chair and smiled at Steve.

"Well, first of all, the Air Force sent a girl along to keep tabs on me and keep me out of trouble. Her name is Charlie, but I've forgotten her last name."

"Oh yes". Ben grinned. "I've heard of her. She works for NASA at Ames Research in Mountain View and is the latest darling of the Air Force. I also hear that she is quite attractive."

"I hadn't noticed," Steve growled.

"No, I bet you didn't." Ben smiled even more.

Ignoring his smirk, Steve continued, "Anyway, she and I wandered through crash sites and hangers looking over the leopards, and I even flew one." Ben sat up in his chair. "But it flew beautifully." Ben relaxed.

"So what conclusions did you reach?"

Steve was quiet for a minute as he looked down at his hands. "Well, my only conclusion is that I have more questions than answers and certainly more questions than I had when I left here on Monday." He looked up at Ben whose expression had become more serious.

"First of all, what are slats?"

Ben leaned forward, put his arms on his desk and peered intently at Steve. "They are devices that are extended during landing and take off to give the plane more wing area." Ben's expression became more serious, as Steve watched his face.

"Could these slats be a cause of the problems?"

"Absolutely not," Ben replied. He sat back in his chair, and a smile returned to his face.

"Okay, then why do the latest models come without them?" Ben didn't respond for a minute.

"The latest versions, the "E" models, are built without the slats because," Ben paused a moment. "They're too expensive to build, and we designed the wing with more area instead." Ben watched Steve's face to see if he accepted Ben's answer. Steve didn't change his expression. After a few minutes, Steve nodded.

"Which version has crashed?" Steve asked.

"Only the earlier models with the slats, but that doesn't mean that the slats are causing the problem. We've only made a few of the "E" models, and they've only been flying for a couple of weeks. When they've been around a while they may show the same problem." Steve thought that Ben was not very convincing.

"Okay Ben. I've got to go home and report in now. We will talk more later." Steve got up and walked to the door.

"Oh before you leave, Mr. Stern asked me to tell you that he would like your report on your trip to Tacoma by Monday. That will give you the weekend to work on it." Ben smiled and waved good by.

"Good grief! Monday. I haven't even decided what I

saw in Washington." Steve said as he walked rapidly to his car. He looked down to the ground and saw a parking place with his name painted on it. With a smile, Steve climbed into his front seat and headed for home.

Steve walked into his home, tossed his suitcase on the couch, took off his coat and tie and fell into his favorite chair. Ellen came into the living room with a drink in each hand. "I thought it was you. Let's go sit out by the pool and talk. She gave him a big kiss and they headed out the patio door.

The two of them picked their favorite spots by the pool and sat quietly for a few minutes. They sat sipping their drinks and waiting for dinner to cook. "I sure don't like it when you're away." Ellen said as she reached over and kissed Steve on the cheek.

Steve smiled. "But I was only gone two days."

"Are you sure it wasn't two weeks?" She grinned and squeezed his hand.

They could just barely hear the phone ring in the kitchen. "Do we need to get that?" Ellen asked.

"Hell no. Let it ring," Steve responded.

In a few seconds the door from the kitchen slid open and their daughter, Carolyn, stuck her head out. "Hey Dad. There's some lady on the phone who wants to talk to you." Steve sat his glass down and reluctantly rose out of his lounge chair. "Okay, I'm coming." Ellen watched him walk into the kitchen and close the door behind him.

"Hi Steve. This is Charlie."

"Hi. What's up?

"I've spent the day with our resident expert in aeronautics here at Ames, and he has some very interesting information for you on the F-87. Could you come up tomorrow and meet with us?" Steve didn't respond. "I think you will want to hear what he has to say before you write your report."

"Well, I'm not getting much help here. Yea, I guess I can come up."

"Good. Fly into San Jose, rent a car and drive to the main gate here in Mountain View. Call me from the gate, and I'll drive out to meet you, so you can then follow me to the wind tunnel area where our office is."

"I know how to get to Ames." Steve growled.

Ignoring his growl, Charlie continued, "Good. Get the earliest flight you can. This meeting may last a while. See you when you get here." All Steve heard then was dial tone. He hung up the phone and walked back out to the patio.

"Who was that dear?" Steve had known that question was coming. Ellen trusted her husband, but there were more and more women now working in the engineering field. Still, one calling him at home in the evening was a bit unusual.

"Oh that's Charlie, a woman that the Air Force has hired to tail me and make sure that I write a good report." Steve knew that his description of Charlie was not accurate, but it would probably be one that his wife would accept. "She's a recent Stanford graduate who knows very little about aircraft design but wants to learn." He didn't think that sounded very convincing either. "She wants me to come up to Ames tomorrow and meet with NASA's chief aeronautical expert. She thinks he has something important to tell me."

"It sounds like she is more than just learning." Ellen said. "And how did she get the name Charlie?"

"She said her real name was Charlene, but she prefers to be called Charlie."

"Hmm---you haven't really told me about your trip. You seem to be pre-occupied with it though."

"Yes, I am pre-occupied. It has puzzled me no end.

44

Nothing I saw seems to fit together. The Air Force maintains that the reason for these crashes is pilot error, and my boss wants me to confirm that. But as we searched what was left of the two planes, it was obvious that it couldn't have been a sudden and deliberate turn by the wingman as the Air Force said."

"We?"

"Yes. Charlie had just arrived and accompanied me on my search." Steve thought it best to continue without dwelling on the point.

"None of the flight surfaces were in the wrong position, and the cockpit controls showed that the pilot was trying to counteract some maneuver that apparently caused the problem. I am thoroughly confused. My flight in the plane showed no problems." He stared off into the hazy, reddish sunset over the Pacific.

"You mean you flew a plane that is known for falling out of the sky?" Ellen set down her glass and stared at her husband. He ignored her concern.

"The plane they gave me to try out was not the same model that has had the problem. In addition, the ground crew chief gave me very little information and my friend, Ben, who designed the plane, said nothing more than he had to. I am not big on conspiracies, but I am beginning to wonder about this." Steve sat back, took another sip on his drink and stared even more deeply into the haze covering the sun as it was disappearing over the horizon.

CHAPTER TEN

Steve sat at the Ames main gate entrance area waiting for Charlie to show up. He wasn't sure that he should have come up here, but he had made the trip and would make the best of it. He stared out the window at the huge dirigible hanger still sitting near to the bay. The largest hanger ever built as far as he knew had been built in the early 1930's to house the Navy's new and large dirigible fleet. Moffett Field, as it was called, had served as the Navy's home base for their blimp aircraft squadrons that patrolled the California coast looking for submarines during World War II.

It was still housing anti submarine aircraft, the PV-3 Orion as he recalled. He was not that familiar with Navy planes, but he thought that was the plane the Navy was now using for anti-sub work. Building such a large hanger was an amazing engineering feat. He was trying to imagine what structure the engineers designed to support such a mammoth building.

"Hi Steve." Charlie burst through the door to the waiting room. "I've got your clearance approved, so follow me to the test area." Steve wondered why she never seemed to let him respond before having something else to say.

He got into his rental car and moved in behind her as she pulled out toward the big hanger. They parked in a big lot, and she motioned him to follow her into the building.

They walked into an office area where Charlie introduced him to the head secretary. She asked them to wait and then ushered the two into a small but plush office. The middle-aged man behind the desk rose, smiled and shook hands. Charlie introduced him as Doctor Frank Evans, the head of the wind tunnel test section at Ames. "Please sit down, both of you. And can I get you a cup of coffee?"

"Black for me please," Charlie responded.

"No thanks," Steve added.

Doctor Evans took the last sip from his cup and gave it to his secretary as she brought in Charlie's coffee. "I've been looking forward to talking with you ever since Charlie told me that you were heading the inspection team searching for the cause of the F-87 crashes. She told me about your trip to McChord and what you did and didn't find there. I think I have some information that may be of use to you, but it will take a while to sort it all out." He sat back in his chair and looked like a professor about to lecture his class.

"You may not know that the original design of the F-87 was tested in our wind tunnel here at Ames. Before I get into that, let's talk some history.

"You remember the first jet fighter jet built in the world, the ME-262 built by Messerschmitt for the Luftwaffe during the war. You may have run into one in the air over Germany."

"Yes, I heard about them, but never saw one."

"It's a good thing, because they were fast and could go over 500 miles per hour but could not break the sound barrier. We in the West were surprised at that fact. They had two jet engines and a slightly swept wing. We were developing the F-80, but it was not ready in time to get it into the war before Germany surrendered. The Germans were definitely ahead of us in airplane, jet engine and rocket design. We had failed to pay attention to our Dr. Goddard in the early 30's and we almost paid a heavy price during the war by not developing his rockets.

"When the war ended, the U.S. and the Soviet Union scrambled to get hands on Germany's best rocket and jet engineers. We were also able to retrieve the results of their wind tunnel experiments and spent many hours reviewing their reports. In short, the Germans had concluded, mistakenly as it turned out, that sweeping the wings back was not important in an airplane in breaking the sound barrier. They also had not figured out how to design a wing shape that would slice through Mach One. In short, Germany had developed a fast operational jet fighter, but not one that could exceed the speed of sound.

"As we entered the cold war, it became obvious that we needed to develop a fighter plane that could exceed the speed of sound because the Soviets were well on their way to doing so. Because of our facility here at Ames, we were involved in the development of our country's early jet fighters.

"To shorten my discussion a bit, The F-80 and F-84 would not fill the bill. Our only hope was in the design of your F-87. Our wind tunnel tests showed that a swept wing was essential, and the F-87 is swept back at 36 degrees. We also found out that the wing cross section of your WW II P-51 was the only wing cross section that could break the sound barrier."

Steve broke in. "Yes--- the laminar flow wing as I recall its name."

"Yes, and it has a remarkably low air resistance or drag at high speed. The P-51 is actually credited with wining the air war over Germany because its low resistance wing allowed our fighters to escort our bombers in their runs over Germany, as you well know."

Steve smiled and nodded. Frank continued. "The laminar flow wing had exactly the characteristic we needed to break the sound barrier, so we built and tested models to confirm our hopes. The tests we conducted here proved the wing's value at trans-sonic speeds.

Unfortunately, the laminar flow wing has one serious flaw. It has very poor lift at low speeds unless the wing's area is significantly increased, which then reduces its ability to break the sound barrier. You might call a paradox of diminishing returns."

"Yea, that makes sense," Steve broke in. "So what did you do to fix the problem?"

"Well, design geniuses in LA added movable slats to the forward edge of the wing. These flap-like structures are about eight inches wide and extend the wing's full length. They move in and out by hydraulic pressure, and when they are extended forward about six inches they provide the lift needed when the plane takes off or lands. They act like flaps, but are on the leading edge of the wing instead of the trailing edge. As you know, there is no room for them on the trailing edge of the wings because of ailerons and flaps. When the slats are stowed at cruising altitude the wing then becomes laminar allowing the plane to exceed the speed of sound.

"It looked like a perfect solution to the low lift problem of the otherwise perfect trans-sonic wing shape. When the plane is taking off, the slats are deployed forward giving the extra wing area and lift needed and then are stowed back in the wing when the plane reaches enough speed for the wing to provide sufficient lift without them. Then the opposite is true as the plane is slowing for a landing,"

Frank said.

"What could be simpler?" Steve was finally able to get a word in. "It is a supersonic wing when flying at high speed and a high lift wing when coming in for a landing or taking off." Steve sat back wondering what the hell this had to do with the problems the F-87, were having with "pilot error" crashes.

"So you are probably wondering what all this wing design theory has to do with the crashes your F-87 has been seeing lately. Well frankly, so am I." He looked over at Charlie. She looked as puzzled as did the two men.

"I have studied your wing design over and over and can find no reason why these slats could be causing the plane to fall out of the sky. When I heard that Charlie was working with you to solve this problem, I thought I would invite the two of you in for a discussion. And there it is." Dr. Evans leaned back and through his hands up in the air. "The rest of this puzzle is up to you two to answer. If I think of anything else to add, I'll call Charlie who will let you know. Until then, and unless you have questions, there is nothing more I have to offer."

Dr. Evans rose and extended his hand. "It is good to meet you Steve, and I wish you the best of luck."

Steve mumbled a thank you, as he and Charlie turned and walked out of his office. "Let's have lunch and figure out what he just told us," Charlie said as they walked out of the laboratory.

CHAPTER ELEVEN

"As I have said before Steve, I'm really glad that you can get into the officers' club".

He took another drink of his beer and smiled at her. "So am I." Charlie took a sip of her wine and looked out the window at the enormous hanger.

"So what would have happened if your designers down south had not added the slats to the wing?" She looked back at him.

"Oh that's easy. The take off and landing speeds would be so great, maybe over two hundred knots, that these planes would be impossible to land and take off safely. They would not be operational jets with their existing wing area, without the slats. Our runways would have to be miles long. On the other hand, if the wing area were increased, the top speed would be reduced, unless someone came up with a new wing cross section design."

Charlie asked, "So do we know anything more after talking to the good doctor of aeronautics than we did before?"

"I don't know Charlie. We need to review what he said and see if anything comes up.

"First of all, do you remember that you pointed out the

slats on the crashed plane we were inspecting at McChord the other day? And do you remember that the new model of the Γ-87 that I flew did not have them? I am getting suspicious that our sergeant major friend may have had a reason to give me that particular plane to fly.

"As I recall, the slat on the crashed plane we were able to see was in its extended position, or take off speed position," Steve added.

"Yes, but we saw only one of the four wings. The other three were so badly burned and crushed that they were not visible," she responded.

"Okay, but we didn't look too closely at the other wing segments because we thought that they would all be the same. I believe that we need to go back to McChord and take another look. I think we can get an afternoon flight to Seattle. Let's give it a try," Steve said.

"Okay, but let's have lunch first. I'm starved." Steve waved for the waiter to come over.

There were two seats left on the afternoon flight to Seattle. Steve put his magazine down, "My boss wasn't very happy when I told him that I would not have my report ready for him for several more days. And neither was my wife when I told her you and I would be flying to Seattle this afternoon." Charlie smiled as she looked out the window at Mount Rainer.

There was no major waiting for them at the airport this time, so they rented a car and struck out south on Highway 5 toward Tacoma. He showed the guard his reserve officer's identification, the sergeant saluted and waved them into the base. They headed to the scrap yard at the end of the base. Steve pulled to a stop, they jumped out and walked quickly over to the area where they had met. It was where the Air Force had stored the remnants of the two F-87's that had collided on takeoff from the base several weeks ago. They walked around the building and saw—nothing.

"Wait a minute. There is nothing here. I'm sure this is where we walked through the wreckage, right over there." Charlie pointed to a spot behind the building. Steve walked around her and over to an empty spot on the ground. "Yes, and there's a small piece of aluminum lying over there. I know this is the place."

They stood quietly staring around the empty lot when a door suddenly opened on the building and a corporal, who looked as if he had just been awakened from a nap, walked up to them. "What can I do for you two?"

"We were here several days ago looking at the wreckage of two F-87 fighter planes that had crashed, and now there is nothing here. Can you tell us what happened to the wreckage?" The corporal obviously didn't like being addressed by a woman. He turned to Steve.

"I don't know anything about no wreckage, but all the aluminum scrap piled here has been removed and sold to a salvage yard." The corporal was not happy about being awakened. Steve and Charlie looked at each other. "Let's go talk to the colonel." Steve turned and led their way back to the car. They got in and drove to the colonel's office.

"I am sorry Mr. Pritchard, but the colonel has gone home for the day. I suggest that you come back first thing in the morning at 9 AM. I will put you on his schedule, and he will be sure to see you then." The colonel's secretary seemed to be too polite. This time Charlie led the way out of the colonel's office. Neither of them saw the secretary pick up her phone before they left the building.

"Steve, I suggest that we drive over to the hanger and see what we can find out."

"Okay."

The hanger looked completely deserted of people although there were several planes sitting in various stages of repair. "Looks like everyone goes home when the colonel leaves. It wasn't like this when I was in the corps." Steve looked around for the master sergeant they had spoken to when they were there last.

He saw a door open up at the other end of the bay as a staff sergeant walked out with a part in his hand. The sergeant looked up and saw the two staring back at him. He changed direction and walked over to them.

"You know that civilians are not allowed in the hanger," he said with a scowl.

"Yes, we know that Sergeant, but I wonder if we could talk to you for a moment, maybe in your office." The sergeant was impressed that someone thought he had an office. "Let's go out into the lobby where you are allowed to be, and we can talk there."

As they sat down in soft chairs, the sergeant said, "I will tell you anything as long as it is not a military secret." Steve pulled out his wallet and showed the sergeant his ID. They sergeant saw "major" written on his card and his attitude changed quickly. "Yes sir, what can I do for you?" Charlie thought that was more like it.

"Dr. Collins and I are here investigating the crashes of the F-87 fighter jets with which you are probably familiar, and we're wondering if you could answer a couple of questions for us." Steve spoke with the authority he was used to using when addressing enlisted men. The sergeant squirmed visibly in his seat and looked around the room.

"Sir, I am not authorized to discuss this issue with anyone."

"Yes I know Sergeant, and I will not quote you or tell anyone I talked to you, but you seem to be knowledgeable about things around here, and we need accurate information. Pilots' lives will depend on us getting it right. Besides, everyone else around here seems to have gone home."

Steve smiled at the sergeant. "You seem to be someone who understands how things work on these fighter jets." The sergeant smiled weakly. "Do you understand how the wing slats deploy on those F-87's out there?"

"Yes Sir. They are moved in and out by hydraulic pressure, and that's about all I know about the subject."

Steve and Charlie looked at each other. "What activates the hydraulic pressure to move the slats?" The sergeant looked down at the floor. "I'm not really sure Sir. Maybe it is something like air pressure or air speed."

They all sat staring at each other in silence for a while. Finally Steve broke in. "Okay. I think that's about all we are going to get here." He turned to Charlie. "Do you have any more questions for the good sergeant here?"

"No Steve, I don't"

"Let's have dinner and we can talk to the colonel in the morning. And don't worry Sergeant, your secret is secure with us." He wasn't quite sure what the sergeant's secret was, but the sergeant seemed happy that their discussion would go no further.

"This is getting stranger and stranger," Charlie said as she finished her first glass of wine. The waiter brought their steaks and Steve motioned for him to fill up her glass. "Yah. Nothing seems to add up," he said as he cut into his blood red meat.

"It's as if they will tell us anything, but we haven't asked the right question yet. You might think that, since they all know what we are looking for, they would answer the questions that we are not smart enough to ask." Steve was enjoying his steak.

"If that's true, then they are definitely hiding something," Charlie added. She hadn't yet begun her meal, still staring out among the gathering clouds at the sun setting over the Olympic Peninsula into the Pacific fog bank.

"What is it that they don't want us to know?"

"Its hard to eat and think at the same time," Steve swallowed another piece of steak.

"Ah yes. You men have a hard time walking and chewing gum. I almost forgot." She cut into her steak, as Steve looked a little embarrassed.

He sat his fork down. "You know what. My friend Ben, back in the design section in LA would know the answer to my question of what activates the hydraulic actuators on the slats. I'm anxious to get back and ask him, but we still need to call on the colonel in the morning. He probably isn't going to answer any questions, but we need to be polite and let him know we were here." He said as he picked up his fork.

"I suspect he already knows we are here," Charlie responded. Steve nodded as he stared into his glass of wine.

Steve paid the bill and they walked out to the car and headed back to their motel. They talked continuously on the ride back, but neither could answer the problem.

They pulled into the parking lot and got out into the cool night air. Walking into the lobby, Charlie looked up at him and asked, "Would like to come by my room and have a night cap before retiring?"

"No thanks, Charlie. I've got to check in at home and figure out what to ask the colonel in the morning." Charlie smiled weakly and waved good night. They each headed in different directions toward their separate rooms.

CHAPTER TWELVE

When they awoke and met in the lobby the next morning, it had obviously been raining hard during the night, but now, it was beginning to let up.

"And a pleasant good morning to you two. How can I help you today?" The colonel motioned for them to sit down while smiling a little more than the occasion required. "The rain has stopped, and the sun is breaking through. Always a good omen here in the state of Washington." The colonel sat back in his soft chair and folded his hands in his lap, waiting for a reply. Charlie and Steve looked at each other each noticing the day old clothes the other was wearing and waiting for the other to begin.

"Well Colonel, we've finally stumbled across some information that makes a little sense, but not totally," Steve began. "The early version of the F-87, the one that is in operation today, has slats running along the forward edge of the wings that, when deployed, apparently give the fighter more lift when it is either descending for a landing or taking off from an airport. These seem to be the only part of the aircraft that could be causing the plane to rotate out of control, but it is not clear how. And why are the slats required anyway? Planes have been built successfully for years without them." Now Steve sat back to wait for a response from the colonel. The colonel rotated his chair and stared out of the window at foggy Mount Rainier. It had some snow left over near the top from the previous winter. After some time, he turned back.

"Charlie, would you mind waiting out in the lobby for a few minutes please? It shouldn't be long." The colonel asked through a thin smile. Charlie stared at him sharply and sat for a moment hoping he would change his mind. Since he was obviously not changing anything, she closed her notebook and slowly rose from her chair looking at Steve. "I will be waiting for you." Steve nodded.

The colonel waited for the door to close then turned to Steve looking more serious than Steve had seen him look before. "Where to start? The colonel moved closer to his desk resting his weight on his arms and his hands clamped tightly together. The medals that he always wore on his left chest were obvious to anyone sitting in front of him.

He stared at Steve scowling. "You will recall that after the war, everyone was frantically searching for the aircraft design that would result in a fighter plane that could break the sound barrier on a routine basis." Steve noticed that the colonel's eyes were now very thin slits below his forehead. He stared intently at Steve as if Steve had broken some highly classified code.

"We were working hard to develop our own, knowing that the Ruskies were possibly ahead in the trans-sonic fighter race, but we had no idea where they stood. Lockheed had built the F-80, but, although it was our first operational jet fighter, it could not break the sound barrier. We continued to search, and this is where your company comes in. It had been developing a transonic fighter, the F-87, since the late 1940's initially with marginal luck. The early task of breaking the sound barrier proved to be very difficult, as you probably remember.

"The first plane to break the sound barrier was not a jet but the rocket propelled X-1 made by Bell Aircraft. Of course it had enough fuel for only two and a half minutes, so, although it provided a great deal of design information, it was certainly of no tactical use."

The colonel shifted his weight. "To digress a bit, you know that the Germans had done considerable work on trans-sonic flight. They did break the sound barrier with their V-2 and developed a jet fighter during the war, but they were unable to combine the two. We gladly grabbed their aerospace engineers when the war ended, in hopes that they could give us the key to the design of a trans-sonic fighter ahead of the Russians."

The colonel again stared out of his window to gather his thoughts. Steve was beginning to wonder what all this had to do with slats on the F-87. He started to ask when the colonel turned sharply back to him and continued his lecture.

"Our German engineers told us about the wind tunnel tests that they had conducted for years that hadn't given them the answers they were searching for. They began by sweeping the wings back a bit to see if that was the key to their search. That proved useful but not conclusive. As the war was ending, they were aiming at the wing thickness, but they had no time to complete their tests before our troops marched into their test labs and carted them back to the U.S. Here, they teamed up with our own engineers, but success was still illusive."

"Yes, Colonel I remember all of that. And what does it have to do with the F-87?" Steve looked at his watch.

"We are getting there. Be patient," the colonel growled.

"When the Korean War started, we came into it with a bunch of World War II propeller-driven fighters that could

59

barely break 400 knots, along with the F-80 and F-84 that were our meager contributions to the trans-sonic air race. We had no idea what we were up against, but we soon found out.

"The swept-wing MiG-15 came screaming out of the skies at us using jet engines designed by Britain's Rolls Royce Company, and we had nothing to compete with or to stand up to them. It could regularly break the sound barrier and fly circles around our World War II fighters. Do you have any idea what that was like? If it weren't for your company coming up with the F-87, we would have been kicked in the butt in the sky over Korea."

Steve opened his mouth, but before anything came out, the colonel continued, "The F-87 is not only a match for the Russian flown MiG-15, it can out-perform it in several areas below 26,000 feet. We did not wipe the skies clean of MiG's, but we stood up to them, but you know all about that, so I won't bore you. My point, however, should now be coming crystal clear. If, for any reason the F-87 should be removed from active service for any length of time, it would be a catastrophe for the Air Force, for United States and for the free world!"

"Just for clarification Colonel, the top speed of the MiG-15 was originally Mach .92. It lost stability when it broke through the sound barrier,"

With a little embarrassment, the colonel continued. "Yes Steve, but its 35 degree swept wing was a design breakthrough that allowed the MiG-15 to exceed Mach 1 at the end of the Korean War. Now the F-87 can also break the sound barrier with ease. Unfortunately, we are now facing a highly advanced Soviet fighter plane that can knock down our B-29 bombers with ease. Nothing we have but the F-87 can stand up to it."

Both men sat back to consider the implications of the

colonel's argument. "What are you saying Colonel? That there is a design flaw in the F-87 that kills our pilots, but that we should ignore it because the only thing keeping the Soviet Union from over running us is the F-87?" The colonel did not reply.

"I am saying that there are times when lives have to be sacrificed to protect our country. We all go to war knowing that death is a possibility." He waited for a response to that, but Steve was trying to grasp the significance of what the colonel had said. Staring down Steve replied quietly, "So where does that leave us?"

"The colonel stood up and stretched out his right hand, "We are both good soldiers Steve and will do what is right for our country. I am anxious to read your report on the cause of our fatal crashes. And by the way, the things we have discussed today are all top secret." Steve, not quite knowing how else to respond, rose, shook the colonel's outstretched hand, turned and walked out.

CHAPTER THIRTEEN

"You look like you've been hit in the face with a wet salmon. What happened in there?" Charlie looked at him with concern. Steve kept his eyes on the road as they headed north toward SeaTac. He did not respond. "Okay, should I guess? He admitted that you have found the problem, but he doesn't want you to say anything about it." Still there was no response from Steve. He gripped the wheel tighter as he stared forward. Charlie decided to keep quiet for the moment, but she continued to look at him intently.

He finally said softly, "Well I guess I can say that we're on the right track."

"Is that all we can say?"

"Maybe I can add that there is more that we need to know before we can write our report." She was startled to hear him say "we" can write the report.

"So what do we know and what do we not know?" Charlie shifted toward him so she could read his body language better. She was getting to know it to the point that he often didn't need to say anything. Today it was telling her that there was more to this issue than either had thought.

"I've got to think for a moment. I'll let you know when I can talk," he said rather roughly. They turned into the rental car return without saying anything.

They had a couple of hours before their flight, so they headed for the bar. They selected a small table away from everybody. Charlie selected a chair from which she could look back at the entrance. They each ordered and were sipping on their drinks before either said anything.

"I am not a conspiracy nut, but did you notice that guy in the Hawaiian shirt as we went through security. He was slightly behind us, but I watched him go through, and show the guard some kind of badge; the guard let him through without the usual search. And he has no luggage," she said with a shrug.

"No Charlie, I didn't notice," Steve responded trying to act interested. Charlie had another sip of her drink. "And guess what. He just entered the bar and ordered a drink. He is sitting at the far end of the room where he can look at us."

"Yes, so are several hundred other people in Hawaiian shirts." Steve obviously had other things on his mind. "You had better keep an eye on him." Charlie ignored his sarcasm.

She turned toward Steve while watching the Hawaiian man out of the corner of her eye. "So are you going to tell me where we are in this mess?"

After a minute and a couple of sips, he said softly not to be overheard, "Well, there is something to the slat theory we uncovered, but I am not sure what exactly it means. It just appears that they are somehow causing the crashes we have been directed to investigate. But there is a lot more to it than that." He paused wondering how much he should tell her.

He slowly reached into his coat pocket, pulled out an envelope and handed it to her under the table. "Here, read this." Charlie took the envelope, opened it and pulled out

63

a piece of paper with a hand written message in large letters. "YOU ARE ON THE RIGHT TRACK. DON'T STOP NOW."

"My God! Where did you get this?"

"It was stuffed into the door handle on my side of the car when we were into the colonel's office. I retrieved it when we got into the car to come up here. I am beginning to think your conspiracy theory my not be far off. Can you still see the Hawaiian guy?"

"Yes. He seems to be reading a newspaper and not paying any attention to us. But why would anyone be following us anyway? We are just trying to find the cause of Air Force plane crashes. It doesn't add up." Charlie answered as she took another sip of her drink, watching their follower intently.

The call for boarding their flight to San Jose finally came over the load speaker so they gulped the remainder of their drinks, picked up their brief cases and headed for their gate. The man in the Hawaiian shirt folded his newspaper and headed for the exit after them. Charlie took a look over her shoulder as they walked down the concourse but she couldn't see anything strange. She took Steve's arm and held on.

They sat next to each other in the coach section in the just under two-hour flight to the Bay Area. He had planned to book a flight straight to LA, but Charlie had asked him to accompany her to San Jose and then transfer to an LA flight. She bent over close to him and whispered in his ear, "Please tell me what else you know that you haven't shared with me. We both know that you're holding back."

"There isn't much more that I can tell," he whispered, distracted by the fragrance of her perfume. "My discussion with the colonel revealed that he probably knows about the slats, but he added nothing about how they operate or why they would be causing the accidents." He paused and looked at her to see if she was buying his partial truths. She wasn't. "Your body language tells me that you are still holding back."

"I've got to do something about my body language."

She squeezed his arm. "You couldn't even if you wanted to." She gave him a big smile that he could only partially see.

"Hey wait a minute. Do you see that man up there in the aisle seat in the blue shirt? Doesn't he look like the guy in the Hawaiian shirt in the Seattle airport?" Steve lifted himself above the edge of the seat in front of him for a better view.

Charlie now strained to see. "Yes but he has on a different shirt, she said."

"Of course he does. That's a favorite trick of private detectives. Wear a bright shirt and change it half way through the chase, so your victim doesn't recognize you. Now you've got me believing that we are being followed." Steve slumped back in his seat as he looked out at Mount Shasta passing below.

She asked, "Where is your car at the airport? Let's split when we get off, and I'll meet you at your car. That should confuse him." Charlie pulled out her parking ticket, and she wrote the number on his calling card. "Now let's try to look innocent as we get off the airplane."

"Maybe we can look like newlyweds," as she squeezed his arm."

"And go in different directions? I don't think so." They both chuckled. Steve noted with surprise that he enjoyed the feel of her body next to him.

They left the plane a few hundred yards apart. Charlie picked up her luggage and walked outside to get the bus to the parking lot. Steve's luggage was on its way to

Los Angeles, so he wandered around the concourse as if he were looking for another flight. He did not see the man in the blue shirt so walked out to the bus entrance and boarded the next bus to the parking lot. He had a hard time reading her handwriting but soon walked up to the beige Toyota that she had described. She was sitting in the driver's seat staring out the window looking terrified.

Steve opened the door and asked, "What's wrong? You look terrible?" She didn't look at him but handed him a piece of paper. "It was on the windshield under the wiper." She could hardly speak. He looked at the paper.

"Be very careful what you do next. The safety of your country and your life are at stake, and when the country's safety is at stake, one or two lives mean nothing," it said.

Steve slumped against the car, continually staring at the paper. Charlie looked straight ahead into the setting sun without blinking.

CHAPTER FOURTEEN

Steve sat nursing a single malt scotch as his wife worked to prepare dinner in the kitchen. It was after dark when his plane from San Jose finally arrived at LAX. His family, including their dog, Rex, all greeted him warmly at the door. He visited with his three kids for a while, but they had homework to do and soon trotted off to their rooms. Ellen brought him a refill and told him that dinner would be ready soon and that the kids had already eaten.

Steve loved to stare up at the stars and try to name them. He had learned celestial navigation as a pilot but hadn't used it much lately. He still remembered his stars in case he ever needed to use his sextant again. Unfortunately, the bright lights from the city interfered, and tonight his mind was not on the stars.

He was thinking about tomorrow and his planned discussion with the chief engineer. "He must know more about the slats than anyone, yet he has told me nothing. Has my old buddy deserted me?" He wondered out loud. Rex, coiled in a sound sleep up at Steve's feet, looked up startled at his master's sudden outburst. Steve reached down and scratched Rex behind his ears as his dog settled back to his evening's nap.

"Above all, what should I tell Ellen?" He looked up at the stars as if they might help him. Steve shivered at a sliver of fog rolling in off the Pacific. "They're no help either." Rex looked up again, but this time with only one eye open.

"Honey, dinner's ready."

Ellen was a masterful chef and this dinner was no exception. "Honey," Steve asked. "What is this young generation going to do when they get married and discover that neither of them can cook?" Ellen laughed and set the steaming hot platter on the table.

"I have often wondered that myself," she said as she reached down and kissed his cheek.

After dinner they sat out under the stars sipping their coffee and watching the fog crawl slowly up the beach toward their home. It was nice now, but the temperature would drop significantly when the fog reached them.

"Ellen, I've got something I want to talk with you about. You know how I value your insight, and I need all of the help I can get on this one." She looked quizzically at him.

"Of course, Honey. Anything I can do to help. Does it have to do with the lady from Palo Alto?"

"No, Dear it does not. Although she is a part of the mystery." Suddenly he could smell Charlie's fragrance on the plane.

Ellen turned toward her husband to listen carefully to what he had to say. "Go on, Honey."

"As you recall, I have been selected by the president of my company to find out why our fighter plane, the F-87, has been crashing around the globe for no apparent reason. To help me solve this riddle, the Air Force hired a consultant to assist me. That's where Charlie, the lady from Palo Alto as you call her, comes in. When we identify the cause of these crashes, we are to write a report together that will clear up the mess and make my company and the Air Force look good. I skipped over the most important part. The Air Force has ruled that all of the crashes were caused by, 'pilot error.' This is standard practice for the Air Force when they don't know what causes crashes."

"So it sounds to me like you two are to write a glowing report exonerating the F-87, get your promotion and then get back to work on your next project. What seems to be your problem with that?

"Oh wait a minute; I think I see. You and Charlie have uncovered the real problem with the plane and are trying to decide whether you should write a report of the plane's problem or whitewash over it and let the plane keep flying. Is that pretty much it?"

Ellen had been a high school math teacher when they met and Steve was impressed with her ability to get quickly to the heart of a problem. She was disarmingly smart and was an excellent teacher but had given up her career to marry Steve and raise their children.

Steve always wondered if she resented giving up her career for him and their family. He was from the old school that believed that a wife should be at home with the kids and not tramping off to work every day. She always enjoyed sharing Steve's discussions about his work and often had important suggestions to make. She was getting into this one.

"Well you've come pretty close, but there are other important issues here. We have reason to believe that the higher ups in the Air Force know the cause of these crashes but don't want the public to find out, and they particularly don't want the Soviets to know. We also have reason to believe that Charlie and I are being followed. We know for sure that Charlie's life has been threatened, but we have no idea who is doing this to us." Steve stopped and again looked up to the stars, but they were still no help.

"My God, Honey, this sounds serious. Let's back up. Do you two really know what is causing the crashes?"

"Well yes and no."

"That's not an answer Steve. I would flunk you for that one in my class." She looked more serious than ever.

"Okay, I will try to clarify that remark. I think I have discovered what device is responsible for the erratic behavior of the planes that lead to the crashes. But I have no idea what causes the particular part of the plane to malfunction.

You see we have to identify both the guilty plane part and the action that is causing it to misbehave." Steve again paused feeling the damp fog roll in as he waited for a response from his wife. She was trying to digest what he was saying before she said more.

"But the conclusion we reach in the report is potentially the real problem. When I find all the answers, should I write a report that embarrasses both the Air Force and my company, or do I write a report that whitewashes the whole thing as you put it? Pilots are dying every week, and maybe I can stop it. Now they have brought in national security, and I've been told that a negative report will endanger our country and make us more vulnerable to attack by the Soviets." Steve was getting red in the face and the veins in his neck were standing out. He leaned back in his patio chair and tried to calm down.

After a few minutes Ellen responded, "I can see why your company and the Air Force might be embarrassed by such a finding, but why would national security suffer?"

He smiled at her. "Unfortunately the answer to that question is 'Top Secret,' so naturally I can't share it with you. You will just have to take my word for it." Ellen had that look that Steve recognized as disbelief. "I haven't even shared that answer with Charlie." He hoped that would calm her down, but no such luck.

"So much in your life lately has been classified 'Top Secret' that I wonder what you are really up to." She spoke softly hoping he didn't hear her. They both sat quietly for a moment as the fog bank now encroached on their property as the temperature dropped rapidly.

Ellen finally spoke up. "Honey, you know that I have a vested interest in your report. If it costs you your job and gets us thrown out of this lovely home, I will be very upset. I have confidence, however, that you will do the right thing." She stood up and headed for the house. "You can join me in bed when you wish." Steve continued to sit now becoming enveloped by the damp, cold fog bank that kept him from looking up at the stars.

"I've got to talk to my buddy Ben, and see what is causing this slats to move." Rex curled up in front of the fireplace as Steve turned out the lights and followed his wife into their bedroom.

CHAPTER FIFTEEN

"Good morning Mr. Pritchard. Please sit down. Ben is finishing up a meeting and will be able to see you in a few minutes." Steve thanked her and sat down in Ben's lobby. He stared out the window knowing that he could see the side door to Ben's office and would know when his meeting was breaking up.

It was a few minutes when the secretary's phone rang and, after saying a few words, she sat it back on the hook and said to Steve, "You can go in and see Ben now Mr. Pritchard. His meeting is over. Steve nodded and rose out of the chair. "That's funny," he thought. "Nobody came out of the only two doors into his office. Hmm.

"Hi Ben, it is good to see you."

"Welcome home, Steve. I hear you've been traveling a lot lately." They both sat down. "Have you found anything, and are you ready to write your report yet?" Ben reclined his chair back and put both hands behind his head.

"Yes Ben, I think I've found a few clues, and each one looks good by itself, but they just don't add up when I try to put them together." He searched Ben's face for any indication of what he was thinking, but Ben retained his continual smile. Each waited for the other to speak.

"Without getting too deep into the details, the only part of the plane that could be causing the out-of-control rotation are the wing slats. Of course the ailerons could be the culprit, but it seem highly unlikely that they are causing the problem." Ben's grin was beginning to diminish. "However, we don't have enough details on how the slats are actuated to reach a conclusion and write our report yet."

"We?" Ben moved forward in his chair and lowered his hands from behind his head.

"Yes. Didn't I tell you about the woman that the Air Force has hired to birddog my search and help me write the report. She works at Ames up north."

"Oh yea, I think I remember something about her." Steve couldn't recall if he had told Ben about Charlie or not, but Ben seemed to agree that he had, so he let it drop. "So is there any way I can help, Steve?" Ben's smile had now completely disappeared.

"Yes, as a matter of fact Ben, there is. As I recall, your group designed the slats and their control mechanism. Isn't that correct?"

"Yes, it's true. In fact I designed the control mechanism myself and am very proud of its operation." Ben rose out of his chair and walked over to one of his cabinets. "I have a drawing of the entire system including a schematic of the hydraulics stored here in my drawing cabinet." Steve noted that it took a special key to open the drawer. Ben spent several minutes thumbing through the drawings. "Here they are." Ben pulled out a handful of blueprints, walked over to his drafting table and laid them out. Steve got up and walked over to the table.

Steve looked down at the drawings then raised his head. "Ben, is it okay with you if I take these to my office where I can look over them at leisure?"

"Sure Steve. Go ahead. Just remember not to take them

out of the plant. They are still classified as you can see by the stamp."

"No worries Ben. I'll take good care of them." Steve rolled them into a bundle, put them under his arm and walked out of the office. "Thanks Ben. See you later." Ben waved a goodbye as his secretary closed the office door behind him.

CHAPTER SIXTEEN

Steve made two stacks of drawings on his drafting table. One stack consisted of drawings that could not possibly be the problem, and the other smaller stack was made up of drawings that might be the problem. For the rest of the afternoon, he went through the "most likely" stack several more times weeding out the most unlikely drawings, one by one. He kept returning to the schematic of the slats' hydraulic system. He traced every line from the pump to the control cylinder, but could see nothing that would cause it to malfunction.

"I've got to go home," he finally admitted to himself, his eyes and logic bleary from hours of staring at the drawings. He folded up the drawing of the hydraulic system, put it in his briefcase, put on his coat and headed for the gate. If he got caught carrying a classified drawing out the gate he could be put in jail for a long time. But he wanted to share the drawing with Charlie. Maybe she could identify the problem.

He got into his car, breathed a sigh of relief and headed out onto the road home. Too tired to talk to his wife, who was sound asleep anyway, he quietly crawled into bed and quickly fell asleep.

The smell of bacon frying woke Steve as he rolled out of bed and into the shower while rubbing his eyes.

"Have you found anything that might help you find the problem, Honey?" She asked as she put a plate of bacon, potatoes and scrambled eggs in front of him. "No Dear, not yet." He dove into his breakfast.

"I am going up to Ames this morning to pick Charlie's brain on the design of the hydraulic system."

"Have you memorized its design?"

"No Dear." Steve looked around to make sure his kids were not in hearing distance. "I have the drawings of the system with me, although don't say anything about it as they are classified and shouldn't be out of the plant." He wiped his plate with his toast.

Ellen stared at him with her hands on her hips. "Isn't that taking quit a chance, Dear?"

"Yes it is Honey, but I'm on the verge of finding the problem and think it is worth the chance." Ellen turned back to put the dishes in the dishwasher.

Steve filled his suitcase, picked up his briefcase and headed for the door. "I hope to be home this evening, I'll call you if I have to spend the night.

"With that suitcase, it looks like you are going to spend a week." Ellen kissed Steve on his cheek as he walked out the door and into a fog shrouded morning.

As he headed north toward the airport, the fog slowly cleared. Steve was immersed in the design of the hydraulic system as he remembered it. He almost ran a red light without thinking. His flight to San Jose went without a hitch, but he still couldn't concentrate on travel. He rented a car and headed north to Mountain View along the Bayshore Freeway. He turned into Ames and called Charlie from the visitor's gate. "Hey. Come and get me. I have something to show you."

"Okay, tell me why you came all the way up here without warning me," Charlie asked as they both walked into her office. Steve closed the door. He reached into his briefcase, pulled out the drawing of the hydraulic system and opened it on her desk.

Her eyes popped open as she read, "Top Secret" stamped on the upper left hand corner of the drawing. "What in the hell are you doing? We'll both go to jail!"

"Calm down and lock your door. I am convinced that the answer we have been searching for lies somewhere on this drawing. We've got to stare at it until we find the cause of the crashes." Steve smoothed out the print so they both could look at it together. Steve noticed that she was wearing that same perfume again.

Charlie sat back in her chair. "Steve, my good friend. You know that I'm an expert in aircraft design but know next to nothing about hydraulics. I have no idea what I'm looking at here." Steve exhaled and sat back. Okay, let's go back to the beginning."

He spent fifteen minutes reviewing what they had found and added the facts of national security and his company's wish to whitewash the whole problem. They didn't want to reveal to the public and the Soviet Union that they had made a mistake in the design of the nation's first transonic fighter plane. "Its logical. The only part of the plane that could be causing it to rotate so violently and unexpectedly are the wing slats, but how are they causing the rotation?" Our job is to find the answer to that problem that I think lies somewhere on this drawing. I just don't see it."

Charlie replied, "Okay, you're the expert in hydraulics, not me. So why did you come up here?" The smell of her perfume was getting intense. He didn't answer. She continued, "Why don't you just explain what we are looking at, and maybe something will come to you while we are at it." She leaned forward to look at his drawing ignoring the classified stamp on it. Her brown hair fell on the drawing, but she brushed it out of the way.

Steve spent several minutes describing each component on the drawing and what it did to activate the slats. Charlie listened intently. When he finished they both stared at the drawing, but neither said anything. Finally Charlie asked, "So tell me again what device begins the sequence to actuate the hydraulic system to move the slats?

"It's this device here, an altimeter, that automatically closes an electrical circuit over here when a pre-set altitude is reached. This circuit energizes this hydraulic pump, forcing oil out to the actuators, which move the slats forward to provide extra lift when the plane is taking off or landing. Ben is proud of the fact that the pilot does nothing to move the slats. They move automatically when the plane reaches a pre-set altitude. A rather ingenious design I'd say."

"And that is when the accidents have happened, at landing and takeoff?"

"Yes, exactly."

They both continued staring at the drawing.

Charlie rose up tossing her hair back. "Okay, I think I am beginning to understand." She paused. "Just one thing. This design is for one wing, but where's the design for the other wing?"

Steve laughed. "Yes silly. This is the hydraulic system for just one of the wings. The other one is exactly like it! Oh my God! That's it! You have solved the problem!" He reached over, kissed her on the forehead, jumped up and pranced around the office punching his arms like he was in a boxing ring. "Let's go to lunch. I'm buying," he shouted as he stuffed the classified drawing back in his briefcase. Everyone in the office stopped their work and stared at them as they walked out of the office.

CHAPTER SEVENTEEN

"Okay wise guy, tell me what we've discovered. You've had your lunch and beer. Now I want you to talk to me before I bash you in the nose."

Steve looked around. "We need to be careful that no one can hear us."

"Baloney Major. We're stashed over in the corner like two star struck lovers, and no one could hear us if I cried for help." Charlie pushed her plate away, folded her arms and glared at him.

"Okay, okay. Just let me finish this last potato chip first. And by the way, what is that perfume you're wearing? Charlie threw up her arms in disgust and tossed her head back.

Steve took a last swallow from his beer mug, leaned back and laid his arms across the table. He wiped his mouth with his napkin and a smile, not a smirk, came across his face.

"Well my dear, think about it. What happens when a wing slat is deployed? The lift on that wing increases substantially, and of course, the opposite happens when the slat is stowed. Obviously the slats on each wing must deploy *exactly in unison,* or there'll be a short period when the plane is out of balance. Am I being clear?"

"So the slats are deploying unevenly. I get it. But why?"

"Each hydraulic system has its own altimeter to actuate its hydraulic pump." Steve paused for effect. He lowered his voice. "Have you ever seen two altimeters that read exactly the same height? I could be holding two altimeters that were exactly the same, one in each hand, and would they read the same? No! Set at 1000 feet, one might read 1005 feet and the other read 995 feet.

"Now think about the effect this small difference would have on plane descending onto or taking off from a runway. A difference of only a few seconds in individual slat deployment would make the plane sufficiently unstable to cause it to rotate violently for a short period. The pilot would be unable to gain control until both slats had completely deployed. In extreme cases, a plane could easily rotate into its partner if they were flying next to each other."

"Or it could cause a plane to crash before the pilot could gain control back," she responded, "And all the problems we've seen could've been caused by what we have uncovered."

"Exactly! And there is nothing that can be done to fix this problem without completely redesigning and grounding all of the planes currently flying. I think I'm starting to see that our problems are just beginning," he added.

They were both quiet for a while staring at each other. Finally Steve spoke up. "You know that our hypothesis won't go anywhere unless we have proof."

"Okay my friend. How do we get proof?"

They were both quiet again. "A test will do it; a test in the environment that caused the crashes. We need to find a vacuum chamber in which we can control the altitude and place two identical altimeters in it to see how they perform," Steve responded. Charlie nodded but didn't say anything. She was obviously thinking.

"I have it. My cousin Billy runs the environmental test lab at Ford Aerospace just a couple of miles up the road in Palo Alto. He owes me a favor. Let me call him," Charlie eventually said. They got up and drove back to her office.

As Charlie was rummaging through her phone book, Steve spoke up. "But how do we get two of the altimeters that are used in the slat control system?" Charlie set her phone book down at looked at him. "Hey! We can solve only one problem at a time." She finally found Billy's number and rang him up.

"Okay, he'll do it tomorrow if we can locate a couple of the wing altimeters. Are we making any headway on that problem?"

"Strangely enough we are," Steve replied. "There's only one Air Force base here in the Bay Area where the F-87's are stationed, and that's at Hamilton in Marin County. I have an old friend stationed there. Let's get in the car. You drive, and I'll enjoy the view over the Golden Gate Bridge."

As they drove out onto the bridge she turned to Steve. "So tell me about this friend of yours at Hamilton." Steve was engrossed with the spectacular view of the bay from his passenger seat. "Look at all those sailboats down there. That sloop is beating hard into the wind on a port tack, and the crew is really getting wet. I wish I were down there with them to let out on the jib sheet a little so it would drive better."

"I didn't know you were a sailor. How long have you done that?"

Steve smiled. "There is a lot you don't know about me, lady. Someday we'll sit down and get to know each other better. Right now we've got to get this problem solved."

Charlie smiled weakly as she kept her eyes glued to the road in front of them.

CHAPTER EIGHTEEN

They were standing next to the hanger at Hamilton Air Force Base. "Getting through the gate was the easy part; now comes the tough one. My friend was my crew chief in England during the war. He recently wrote me that he had been stationed here as his last posting before retirement. I hope he hasn't retired, or this trip will have been in vain."

They walked into the meeting room in the hanger There was no one to greet them, nor was there any way to get farther than the locked door leading into the hanger. As they stood there staring at the door, someone came through it and looked startled to see two civilians standing there. "Can I help you?" he asked.

"Yes, if you would please. We're looking for Master Sergeant Bob Phillips. Do you know him?"

"Sure I know Bob. He is working inside right now. Do you want me to get him for you?"

"Yes, if you would, please."

"Sure. And who shall I tell him wants to see him?"

"Please tell him that Major Steve Pritchard is here."

The young man with corporal stripes in his arm snapped to attention and replied, "Yes Sir. I'll get him right now." He turned and waked out the door.

The two sat down and waited.

"Now remember to say nothing and smile continuously at him. Men like that. And you can offer to get me a cup of coffee if you wish," he said jokingly.

"Yea. Fat chance of that happening," she chuckled.

Shortly the door burst open and out walked a middle-aged master sergeant. "Major! How the hell are you?"

"I'm just fine Sergeant. And how are you doing?" They shook hands warmly.

"Well I'm only a couple of weeks from retirement so that makes me feel good. Boy its great to see you." He sat down next to them. "But what brings you to Hamilton?"

"First let me introduce you to my lab assistant here, Charlie. She's working with me on a classified project having to do with the F-87." Charlie smiled at the sergeant and then glowered at Steve.

"You may remember that I work for Western Aviation, the company that builds the jet. They have asked me to check out something on the slats operating mechanism, so I thought of you. Maybe you can get me the part I want."

"Hmm. Okay, what part do you need?

"Well Sergeant, we need a couple of the altimeter devices that activate the hydraulic system on the slats."

The sergeant rubbed his chin and thought for a minute. "Why do you want them Major?"

Steve was stopped. How should he answer that? "Our design department asked me to check on their operation by testing out a couple in the field. Do they activate at the proper altitude? I am not sure exactly why they want to know this. They don't tell me everything. Classified you know." Steve stared at his old friend hoping that his answer was believable.

The sergeant rose. "Wait here Major. I think I can find a couple for you. You did want two, right."

"Yes Sergeant. Two would be fine." Steve tried to look calm although his heart was racing. The sergeant walked out closing the door behind him.

"So, since when have I been demoted to lab assistant?" Charlie shoved an elbow into Steve's ribs.

"Hey stop that. You'll get a promotion when we get out of here."

"Sure, as long as I get your coffee. I didn't get my PhD to get you coffee!" The door opened.

"Here you go Major. I put them in a paper bag so they wouldn't be too conspicuous. Don't forget to return them; I don't want anything to interfere with my retirement."

"Don't worry Sarge. I'll have them back within a couple of days."

The two walked out holding their breaths. "That was well done, Major. Now let's get back to Palo Alto.

"So you think I don't know much about you, right Steve?" He was entranced with the view of the bay as they crossed the Golden Gate back into San Francisco. He looked to his right toward Japan and the fog bank that seemed to be continually hanging out over the Pacific and then turned to her and smiled.

"You know who gave the Golden Gate its name?" He was not responding to her question, but seemed to have his own agenda. "No, not many people know that it was John Charles Fremont who was sailing on his way home from battling the Mexican forces in Santa Clara Valley. On his way back to his base in Marin County in 1856 or '57, he noticed the sun setting through the gate and is said to have remarked, 'Look at that Golden Gate.' The name stuck."

Charlie was obviously not as impressed as he thought she should be

"The first thing I know although it is not about you, is that Stanford beat your alma mater, UCLA, by three touchdowns last Saturday. And when we beat Cal next Saturday in the Big Game, we'll be headed to the Rose Bowl." She had an intolerable smirk on her face as he turned back to look at her. "We haven't lost a big Game in three years so it ought to be a cinch. As I recall, the Rose Bowl is not too far from where you live. Do you want to go? I'll get you a ticket,"

That was the last straw. "In the first place, how do you know that I went to UCLA, and in the second, beating Cal will be no cinch, not by a long shot. UCLA is not Cal, but we are cousins, so I will happily take a bet on the Big Game."

"To answer your first question," she responded, "I not only know that you went to UCLA, I know all about your service in World War II, especially the part you played in getting the P-51 operational."

Steve put his arm back on his seat as he turned completely toward her. "Oh you do, do you?"

"Yes. Do you want me to tell you the story?"

"I have a feeling that I am going to hear it no matter how I answer that one."

"Yes you are. First of all, you were selected to be the pilot to fly the first operational P-51 that came off the assembly line in 1941. No one in your company knew how a fighter plane designed in England and built in the US would perform, or even it would get off the ground."

"So wait a minute. How do you know that the Mustang was designed in England? My company has always expressed great pride in designing the best fighter built in World War II. Now you're trying to tell me that it was designed by the Brits." She looked over at him, but now he had a smile on his face.

"Okay smarty. You know as well as anyone that the Brits were probably the best aircraft designers in the war.

They only let your company do the final design and build their ultimate fighter plane, because they didn't have sufficient design or manufacturing capacity in England to do it."

Now Steve's smile was gone. "Yes, you're right. And when our Air Corps saw the first one roll off our assembly line they said that no way were they going to let the Brits have it. So it got mysteriously diverted into our Army Air Corps. I often wondered what the Brits thought of that.

"But you are right. When I saw that wing design, I knew that it flew in the face of everything we had learned in flying school, no pun intended," he added.

"Yes, very funny." she said. "We studied that wing cross section at Stanford and did wind tunnel tests at Ames to verify that it could actually approach the sound barrier. And it did all it was designed to do and more. What did they call it, a laminar flow wing? Wasn't it verified at the Cal Tech test labs during the war?"

"Yes, and we used that design in the F-87 that, combined with the new swept wing concept, allowed it to break the sound barrier easily. The reduced drag not only increased the speed of the P-51, it allowed it to fly farther, much farther, than any other fighter plane. It greatly influenced the outcome of war." Charlie waited for him to continue, but Steve stopped talking and looked out the window at the beauty of San Francisco Bay.

"So now do I have to bring up the issue that got you into all kinds of trouble?" Charlie asked.

Steve looked over at her and his face began to get red.

"Do I have to re-live that one?"

"Why not? It showed that you were dedicated to getting the best possible fighter operational, regardless of whose toes you stepped on."

"Thanks for your good words, but it didn't seem like

that at the time." Steve hunched down in his seat and looked straight ahead. His smile turned into a serious stare.

"I know what you must have gone through, but the record is very short on details. You didn't share much with the press. How about telling me?" She slowed down as they drove onto the streets of San Francisco approaching the Marina heading south.

Steve was quiet for a while and then started slowly. "So far you are accurate, but, although the Brits did come up with the initial design concept, we completed the final design and put the finishing touches on the plane's construction drawings. Those of us who worked on it were very impressed with what the Brits had done. Apparently they had combined the best of the Spitfire and the ME-109 into the ultimate fighter plane. We knew it was going to be a winner.

"However, when I finally flew it, as you so accurately describe, it was obvious that it was no match for our opponent, the ME-109. Oh, it performed beautifully below 15,000 feet or so, but above that, it could not do the job. And, of course, we could not always coax the Germans into coming down to 15,000 feet to fight, so something had to be done."

Steve watched the sailboats glide by the Marina and then looked over at Charlie. "I had flown the Spitfire and knew its characteristics and, after I had landed my first flight in the P-51, I walked across the tarmac into the flight commander's office. 'Sir,' I think I said. 'This has the potential to be the best fighter plane ever built. But it needs a new engine. The Allison that was designed into it will not do the job. It needs the Rolls Royce Merlin built in England or it will be a complete dud.'

"I can remember the General looking at me as if I had spit on his lunch.

"Are you crazy? The Allison is built by General Motors, the biggest car company in the US, and you are suggesting that we junk it and replace it with a British built engine," the general snorted. I just stared at him.

"The merlin has a supercharger that will allow it to perform well over 30,000 feet. Maybe the Allison will have one some day, but we need this fighter in Europe now. You must decide. Do we put this spectacular plane in operation now, or do we let more B-17 crews get shot down over Berlin? It's your decision General.' I sat there for a minute looking at the general. I finally got up and headed to the door. 'Remember, the Merlin is now also built in the US by the Packard Motor Car Company,' I said. I smiled as I continued toward the door. I heard him pick up the phone as I walked out. It wasn't long before the first P-51 rolled off the assembly line with a Merlin in its nose.

"Yes, I was proud of what I had done, but I didn't make myself very popular in the offices of General Motors. Yes, there are lots of people who don't care much for me. As I used to say, don't give me a job you don't want done.

"A naval officer friend of mine once told me that Admiral King, who was called up by President Roosevelt to be the Commander in Chief of the U. S. Fleet when the war started, had a reputation for being a real bastard. No one who worked for him liked him. He was considered to be the most disliked officer in the war behind only Britain's General Montgomery.

"At a press conference he attended soon after he took his new job, a reporter asked him about his unsavory reputation. He is reported to have responded, 'When they want to get a job done, they call on the sons of bitches.' The conference was ended on that note. I don't consider myself a son of a bitch, but I don't spend a lot of time worrying about stepping on someone's sensibilities either, not even the president of General Motors. I also understand that it's now the most popular motto in the Navy."

"But returning to the design of the P-51," Charlie responded. "All that combined with the variable pitch propeller made it the best fighter plane ever built and made you a double ace." She looked over at him with a smile. "But maybe your flying skills contributed to it."

"If you wanted to see the fur fly, you should have been there when the Army Air Corps asked me to evaluate their new P-38. It was having real problems when it first came out, and the same Allison engines caused most of them. Without going into detail, when I gave them my summary report saying that they should exchange the Allison for a Merlin, I thought the world was coming down on me. I had calls from senators demanding my resignation, but I survived thanks to several good friends in high places. Needless to say, the P-38 continued to use the Allisons."

CHAPTER NINETEEN

"These two are my guests," Billy told the guard standing at the test lab door. The guard nodded and opened the door for them. It was a change room. "You will need to put on these lab coats and shoe slip-covers. They probably aren't needed, but it makes us look like a real laboratory." Billy opened the door for them as they walked into a beautifully clean and well-lit test lab filled with various test equipment and lab assistants scurrying around.

Steve took Charlie by the arm and pointed to one of the lab assistants. "There is an example of your new job."

"Ha! Very funny. So when do I get my promotion?" They both laughed.

"Okay you two, pay attention!" Billy led them over to a medium size bell jar vacuum chamber. The jar was raised off its base and the two altimeters were suspended above the base with electric wires protruding from each and running to feedthroughs in the base. "I have connected the two altimeters electrically as they would be connected in flight to theses two light bulbs over here, except that the voltage is 110 AC instead of the voltage in the aircraft, the value of which I have no way of knowing. But that doesn't matter, because, as you have told me, all you want to know is at what altitude the circuit opens."

Steve and Charlie traced the circuit through the wall of the bell jar and up to two light bulbs sitting on a workbench. "First I'll energize the circuit by turning on the main power switch here." Billy turned on a light switch, and the light bulbs became bright. "The bulbs are on, because the circuits are closed. I assume that they will open when the pre-set altitude is reached." He smiled as he motioned a technician to set the glass jar onto the base. He reached for a stopwatch on the workbench.

"You told me Charlie that what you want to know is the time difference between when each altimeter opens its circuit as it reaches its pre-set altitude. So, Steve you watch the left light bulb, and Charlie watch the right one. As soon as your light bulb turns off, sing out. I will start the stopwatch when I hear the first shout and stop it when I hear the second. The watch should then tell us the difference that you are looking for. According to the readings on the face of the altimeters, they are both set to open at five hundred feet, and I have set the climb rate in our vacuum chamber at one thousand feet per minute. Something should happen in about thirty seconds. I realize that the climb rate for most fighter jets would be higher, but this will give us a good idea of what you are looking for."

Billy reached over and hit the start button on the vacuum pump as they all heard a chugging sound coming from the pump. The three stared intently at the two light bulbs. Suddenly Steve shouted out, "now," and in a few seconds Charlie answered with her own shout. Billy reached over, turned off the vacuum pump and looked down at his stopwatch. "Three point five seconds," he said as he wrote the figure down on a piece of paper. Steve and Charlie looked at each other. "Okay, but that is just once. We've got to run this test at least two dozen times to get the mean time and standard deviation.

After twenty-five runs, Charlie and Steve found a couple of chairs to sit in while Billy ran his calculations on his brand new hand held calculator. "Just got this thing and am anxious to try it out," he said. He punched in the numbers and then pushed the "Mean" button. "What does it say Bobo?"

Billy glared over at her obviously not happy at being called by his boyhood nickname. "3.65 seconds, with a standard deviation of," he pushed another button, "0.25 seconds. That's a pretty tight deviation indicating, as you probably remember from your statistic course, that there is not a lot of variation from the mean. These altimeters are pretty consistent."

"Yea, they are pretty consistently wrong. They should activate simultaneously or the wings will have differential lift for what, 3.65 seconds on the average." Charlie said biting her lip as she looked over at Steve. He was staring out into space.

"Okay, you need to explain what you mean," Billy sat down next to them. There were several minutes of silence. Charlie let Steve take the lead.

"We're on the trail of a serious malfunction in the wings of one of our fighter planes." Steve finally replied slowly. "You've been a big help in our search, but we can't reveal any more to you now." Steve stood up and started toward the door as the technician handed him the two altimeters from the bell jar. Charlie got up and followed him into the change room. "Now its back to Hamilton to return these two altimeters."

They sat in the waiting room waiting for Master Sergeant Phillips when the door to the repair end of the hanger opened suddenly and out walked Bob with a scowl on his face. "Here are the two altimeters you loaned us Sarge, as promised." Steve's smile did nothing to cheer up Sergeant Phillips.

"Boy, you guys sure got me into trouble. You didn't tell me that you were being escorted by the FBI."

Steve and Charlie looked at each other. "What are you talking about Sarge?"

"Those two guys who came in about fifteen minutes after you two left with my altimeters. They sat me down and demanded to know what you two wanted, and they threatened my retirement if I didn't tell them. What the hell are you up to?"

"Well, in the first place, we are not spies so I don't know why the FBI is following us. In the second place we didn't know we were being followed by anyone. In the third place, I 'm really sorry we got you into this," Steve lost his smile.

"What did they ask you, Sargent," Charlie replied with a more relaxed voice.

"Well they wanted to know what I knew about what you are doing. Of course I told them that I knew nothing, which is true. But they didn't stop there, implying that I was a part of some conspiracy against the Air Force."

"Yea, they can be pretty intense," Steve was calmer now. "Were you able to convince them of your innocence?"

"Yea, I think so. But they said they'd be back after you two returned to ask more questions."

"Well you can tell them that we returned your altimeters, and went on our way," Charlie jumped in.

"Sorry Sarge. We had no idea this would happen to you." Steve shook the sergeant's hand firmly and gave him a big smile and turned to Charlie motioning her out the door with him.

"Might as well sit here and wait. They'll be here soon." The sergeant sat down and stared at the floor as the other two left the hanger waiting room.

"Should we park the car around the corner and see who drives up?"

"Naw," Steve responded. "They're too smart for that. They'll wait until we are gone. Besides, I don't want them to think that the sergeant told us anything." She started her car and they drove toward the gate.

CHAPTER TWENTY

"So what do we know?" Charlie glanced quickly out over the Golden Gate Bridge as the sun was setting to the west over the Pacific. Steve was looking down at the bay, but most of the sailboats had headed for port.

Steve started slowly. "We know that the F-87 has a serious flaw that causes it to crash periodically. The flaw is in the design of the wing slats because each one is activated separately by its own altitude sensing device." He paused for a moment. "Anyone who is familiar with vacuum gauges knows that no two will read the same at any given altitude, which normally has no serious consequences, but when they are activating devices that give a wing extra lift, the results can be fatal." They were both quiet for a while.

"There is one thing I don't get, Steve. Why don't all the planes crash? Only a couple of dozen are on record as having trouble. Shouldn't they all show the same malfunction?"

"Our problem is that we have tested only one set of gauges. In a perfect world we would test about fifty pair to get a reliable test sample. If we could do that, we would probably find that most are pretty accurate, but this is the only reading we have, and the results show that these vacuum gauges that will be installed on the F-87's will be out of balance for over three seconds on its approach or as-sent if its rate is one thousand feet per minute, a relatively slow rate for most jets.

"But to answer your question, I assume that once a pilot has experienced this problem when landing or tak-ing off, he will increase his dive/assent rate to decrease his time in the unstable condition. In other words, he will fly through it as fast as he can. The problem comes when a new pilot just out of training school, or even an expert in a new aircraft will not be familiar with the problem and will be surprised by the sudden rotation caused by the uneven lift. And if he is near the ground, or if two planes are flying close together, the results could be catastrophic. I would like to have fifty pair for your cousin to test, but that won't happen."

They were both quiet for a while as darkness descend-ed. Neither wanted to bring up the obvious next issue. "So why are we being treated like saboteurs? Why are our con-tacts being given the third degree? Oh my God! My cousin. Do you suppose that he has gone through what the sergeant has had to endure?" She looked at Steve.

"Keep your eyes on the road, and yes, I suspect he has. You will need to call him when we get back and apolo-gize."

"So answer my question wise guy. Why are we treated like Russian agents?"

"I can only speculate, but if we write an accurate report that identifies the real problem is not 'pilot error,' my com-pany will be forced to take the F-87 out of service while the wing problem is fixed. This will be a big embarrassment to my company and will rob the Air Force of its primary transonic fighter plane."

"The Air Force can't be sued, can it?"

"No, that's not possible, but I heard somewhere that a company that makes a faulty product for the government that kills people in the service can be sued. I'm not sure about that, though."

"So what are we going to do, my friend?" Charlie asked.

"I don't know yet, but I need to get more information from my company before I do anything. Get me to my car at Ames so I can fly home and talk some more with people at my company. Then you and I can talk again."

Charlie found it hard to hide her disappointment. "I have an alternate proposal for you this evening big guy. You can postpone your flight for a few hours out of San Jose and I will take you to dinner. Don't look at me like that. I'm paying."

"Wow, I'm being taken out to dinner. This is no doubt a romantic, secluded spot in the hills behind Palo Alto known only to Stanford grads."

"Ha! Don't you wish. No, it's my favorite restaurant in San Jose that will absolutely knock your socks off while taking your mind off of all your troubles."

"I can't pass that up. What's the name of the upscale restaurant if I might ask?"

"I'll tell you only if you promise not to change your mind when you hear it."

"Now I'm intrigued. Please tell me. I can't stand the suspense."

"Mm, not just yet. But I'll give you a hint. It is in the center of old San Jose and has the same name as a famous restaurant in San Francisco. It also has been here for many years. I can tell by looking at you that you still have no idea." They turned into a public parking lot off of First Street.

"They don't even have concierge parking I see."

"Stop being such a fussbudget or I won't take you out again." They stepped out of her car, and she put her arm in his. "That's it right across the street, Original Joe's."

He scanned the building and the street as they walked across it toward the restaurant. "Well, it certainly is the old part of town. Are we going to get mugged by that homeless woman over there? Charlie removed the purse from her shoulder, took out several bills, walked over to the woman and handed them to her. The woman showed an almost toothless smile and thanked her. Steve followed Charlie over and gave the homeless woman several more bills. She thanked him and folded the money in her pocket. She reached into her shopping cart, pulled out a worn out sweater and slipped over her shoulders and continued pushing it down the street.

Charlie put her arm back in Steve's, looked up at him and smiled as they headed back toward the restaurant. "Did you do that because I did?

"I can imagine why you might have thought that, but no my mother taught me to give what I have to the homeless many years ago. It sometimes irritates my wife when I do that as we walk along Skid Row in LA. She thinks that they will just go out and spend it on drugs or liquor. My response is, so what? Let's concentrate on eating. I'm starved.

"What are all these people standing out here on the street? They seem to be blocking the entrance."

"Those are customers waiting to get a table at this fabulous establishment."

"You mean that we have an hour wait?"

"Not on your life Bucko. Follow me!"

"Hi Paul. We're going to eat at the counter" Charlie smiled and waved at the maître de. He waved back and returned her smile. She navigated Steve through the waiting crowd over to the almost-empty counter. "Grab a stool anywhere and get ready for an old fashioned Italian dinner like you probably had as a kid."

The noise was almost deafening as pans rattled, plates clanked and people sitting at the tables talked incessantly. The two were facing the kitchen just across from the counter where six specialty chefs were each facing his own stove cooking his own part of the meal. Steve was amazed. It seemed like mass confusion in front of them. Not only were the chefs tossing a frying pan in each hand, but also a dozen waiters were moving rapidly back and forth behind them relaying orders to each chef. Steve was mesmerized.

"Wow, this is really something! Look down at the end of the line. The first chef is frying steaks and chops, and that's all he does. When a waiter shouts out an order for a medium-rare New York, the chef selects one that is perfect, puts it on the plate and sets it up on the counter. Now the waiter picks up his order, walks to the potato cooker and scoops up some French Fries. He then continues on to the vegetable chef in front of us and scoops up the vegies as the next chef pours out a dish of raviolis covered with Italian sauce. This is some operation." He didn't hear the grinning waiter standing in front of them asking for their order.

"Oh, I'd like veal scaloppini with a side of raviolis."

"And I'll have the liver and onions with a side of scaloppini, and let's have a bottle of Chianti."

Steve couldn't take his eyes off of the chefs on the other side of the counter as they waited for their food. No one stopped to rest as they hustled back and forth cooking their specialties. "I've never seen an operation like this. Just watching the operation is worth the price of admission."

"Yes, especially when I'm paying."

Steve put his arm around her shoulder and gave it a squeeze just as the waiter arrived with their dinners. "Wow!

It will take me a week to eat all of this."

"Yea, that's the plan my friend," Charlie murmured under her breath.

They finished their dinner and waddled back to her car. She drove him to the airport and he fell asleep as soon as the wheels left the runway.

"So how did it go up north?" Ellen asked as she handed Steve his gin and tonic. Did you find what you were looking for?"

"Yes, basically I did. Now I'm trying to decide what to do with the information. It's not quite as simple as you outlined the other day. The consequences are a lot more serious, but I can't give you the details just yet, if, in fact, ever. I've got a lot of thinking to do."

"That's okay Honey. I will go in and fix dinner while you finish your drink."

"I ate at the airport while waiting for my flight, but you can fix dinner for you and the kids." Steve sat mulling over in his mind the things he had been through today. When he arrived home, he had a phone call from Charlie telling him that her cousin, Billy, had been through the same type of harassing interrogation that the sergeant had been through. As he sat there, the back gate opened, and in walked his daughter, Jennifer. "Hi Honey. Where have you been?"

"Oh I've been studying with a friend." She smiled, put her books down, walked over to the patio door and looked at her mother in the kitchen fixing dinner. She closed the patio door, walked back to the pool and sat down next to Steve.

"Dad can I talk to you for a minute?"

"Sure Honey, what's up?" He couldn't help but notice that she looked more sixteen than thirteen.

"Well, I'm not sure exactly, but mom has been acting kind of funny lately."

Steve sat his drink down and looked at her with a frown. "Like what Honey?"

"Well when you are gone like you have been the last few weeks, she gets on the phone and makes a call. Sometimes when I walk into the room, she stops talking, or says words on the phone that do not make sense until I leave. She goes out at night saying that she's going to the library, or something. And then she comes home long after the library is closed. I don't know what's going on ---" Jennifer's voice faded into uneasiness. Then she rose up, kissed her father on the cheek, picked up her books and headed into the house.

"Thanks Honey, but I think everything is okay. She is probably just---." Jennifer had disappeared into the house before Steve could finish. He picked up his drink. "I've got to concentrate on my F-87 problem now. I don't need anything else on my mind. This gin tastes good. It wouldn't be hard to be an alcoholic." He leaned back and looked up at the stars.

CHAPTER TWENTY-ONE

As he walked into Ben's outer office Steve smiled at Ben's secretary. "Hi Bev. Is Ben available?"

"Well hello Mr. Pritchard. Let me see." She picked up the phone and said a few words. "He'll be right out Steve. He is finishing a phone call." Steve saw a red light blink on her desk phone. He sat down to wait. In a couple of minutes, Ben came out of his door throwing his suit coat on.

"Wow! You don't need to put your coat on for me Ben," Steve jumped out of the chair.

Ben smiled. "Its not for you my friend. Mr. Stern wants to see both of us in his office." He put his arm around Steve's shoulder and they headed out the door. "I'll be back in an hour or so," Ben said to his secretary on the way out. Steve was a little shocked at Ben's unusual show of affection.

They sat in the comfort of Mr. Stern's outer office chatting about the weather and their common alma mater, UCLA. "Yea, those dummies lost to Stanford in a game that should have been theirs." Mr. Stern's secretary picked up her phone then turned to the two men, "You can go in now gentlemen." She smiled a rather benign smile and returned to her typing.

"Come in you two. I've been expecting you." Mr. Stern leaning back in his chair as the two sat down. "So Steve, Ben tells me that you've been snooping around the design of his slats and their actuating devices. Have you reached any conclusions?" Steve thought it was interesting that Mr. Stern used the word "snooping."

"I came in this morning to talk with Ben about the design of the actuating device, yes. But I am nowhere near a conclusion until I get more data." Steve knew his response was only partially true, but he was concerned about Mr. Stern's rather combative tone.

"Yes, I believe that I am hot on the trail of a design problem that may be causing the problem. Actually I should have said we. Charlie has been a big help." He noticed that Mr. Stern showed a little smile, or was it a smirk?

Mr. Stern rotated his chair toward the window that looked out over the plant, and then rotate back. He was not smiling any more. "Steve, I think we had better have a one on one conversation about this. Ben, would you please wait in my outer office for a few minutes?"

"Of course Mr. Stern," he said as he rose and left the room.

There were a few moments of silence, as Steve grew more fidgety in his chair. Mr. Stern turned to him. "Steve, let me put this to you straight. Our country and our company have a lot invested in the P-87. As you know, the Soviets took the lead when they came out with the MiG-15 a few years ago during the fight in Korea. The Commies hit the scene with an almost supersonic fighter plane that we could not begin to combat. The F-80 and F84 were no match for it. Certainly none of our leftover World War II prop driven fighters could match it."

Mr. Stern rose from his chair and began to walk around his office. "The outcome of the Korean War was in jeopardy, and our company was asked to step into the breach." He stopped at the window and looked out at the buildings with his hands clasped behind his back. After a few minutes, he turned and continued.

"Fortunately, Western Aircraft Company was there ready with a fighter plane that could meet and exceed the enemy's capabilities." Steve thought he was sitting in a locker room at a half time presentation by the coach when his team was behind.

"As you know, we'd developed the laminar flow wing during the war that, not only performed beautifully, but was our entry into the transonic flight world afterward." Steve noted that Mr. Stern gave no credit to the British for their contribution to the wing's design. "In a relatively short time, we were able to adapt German wind tunnel test data with our own experience, and, using the swept wing concept, built a plane that could out-fly and out-maneuver the MiG." He sat back down in his chair and stared at Steve for a moment.

"In short, we have built the only fighter in the world that can stand up to the MiG-15. Do you know what that means?" He sat back in his chair and put his hands behind his head.

"Yes sir. I think I do." Steve had trouble saying anything.

"No, I don't think you do. Think for just a moment what would be our first line of defense against enemy bombers if the F-87 were grounded, for any reason? If the Soviets found out that there was a design problem with our only transonic fighter, we could be facing disaster. Envision a stream of enemy four engine bombers heading south out of Siberia toward Los Angeles, escorted by MiG-15's and loaded with atomic bombs capable of wiping both Seattle and San Francisco on their way south, with nothing available to stop them. Why couldn't we scramble an interceptor group? Because all of the fighters we had were grounded due to a design flaw." Mr. Stern leaned forward and glowered at Steve. A few minutes passed.

"That's the main problem, of course. But let's next consider the results to our company. If you were to identify a design problem that would ground our entire fleet of F-87's, what would our customer, the Air Force, think of us? Do you think they would buy any more fighter planes from Western Aircraft, the company that won World War Two? Yes, you flew the P-51's, but do you think they would remember that?

"We have two problems here, the security of our country and the future of our company. But there is a third problem. What do you think your future would be in a company that had no more contracts? Promotion would be impossible and, in all probability, there would be no jobs left for any of us.

"So I have to conclude that an awful lot rides on the report that you and Charlie are going to write."

"Yes Sir, I think I see what you mean."

"I hope that you do, because, as I say, an awful lot depends on it, for the country, the company and for your future." Steve nodded, rose out of his chair and offered his hand. Mr. Sterns shook it warmly. "The Air Force has asked for it within a week. Do you think that's possible Steve?"

"I think so Mr. Stern."

"Great! That's what I want to hear." Mr. Stern rose and walked over to Steve and put his arm around his shoulder. "And by the way, I think that the corner office over there will just about fit your new job." Steve smiled and nodded. "So let's talk about your future here at Western Aircraft soon."

CHAPTER TWENTY-TWO

"So let me pour you a cup of coffee Steve. You look stunned." Steve sat down in front of Ben's desk while Ben poured him a hot cup.

"Wow, I just had some lecture. He laid it out to me without any confusion or misunderstanding." Steve took a sip from the steaming cup.

"So what do you think?" Ben took a sip on his cup. "You and I have shared a lot of coffee together over the years my friend. I remember you coming into my office in England just after you shot down your fifth Messerschmitt and were suddenly an ace. As I recall, you said it didn't feel any different than having shot down only four, but now you were somebody. Do you feel like somebody today, Steve?"

"Hell, I feel like the weight of the world is on my shoulders, Ben. What's that old saying, I just came in to drain the swamp and find myself up to my ass in alligators." He sat down his cup. "I still have some questions to ask you though. Are you aware of the problem with the wing slat actuators?"

Ben looked down at his half full cup. "As you know, Steve, I designed that actuator system myself. Imagine my plight when I had to go up to Mr. Stern's office after several hundred F-87' had been built and tell him that we had a problem." His response seemed to answer Steve's question partially, but he didn't pursue it. Ben shifted gaze up to the ceiling of his office.

"Did you notice, Steve, that the F-87 you flew up at McChord didn't have slats?"

Steve looked at him with surprise. "Yea I did, but it didn't register with me." He wondered how Ben knew about his test flight at McChord.

"There was a reason besides your safety that the only fighter available for your test flight was the latest model. But could you tell the difference in wing design and in the planes performance?"

Steve thought for a moment. "Yes, there were no slats and the wing cord was thicker, I presume to compensate for the fact that there were no slats. So tell me Ben, what is the purpose of the slats? I think I know, but I'd rather hear the straight scoop from you."

Ben set down his half empty cup and looked up at Steve. "As you know, the P-51 was the pre-curser to the F-87 especially in its wing crossection. But there were a couple of other major differences. To break the sound barrier, we had to sweep the wings back to thirty-five degrees while still using the laminar flow shape; in the process we reduced the chord a bit increasing the aspect ratio. These changes allowed the F-87 to break the sound barrier, although not by much. However, in our wind tunnel tests at Cal Tech, we learned to our horror, that the changes we made, although allowing our new fighter to break the sound barrier, had terrible lift at landing and takeoff speeds. We tried everything we could think of but nothing gave us the lift we needed until I thought of movable slats."

Ben stood up and walked over to the coffee pot as he continued. "The plane needed increased wing area at landing speeds and decreased area at transonic speed. There was no apparent answer until I came up with the idea of expandable slats." Ben turned toward Steve. "I think it was and is a great idea. But, unfortunately, great ideas don't always work as planned. So what do we do? Pull all of these spectacular fighters out of service and expose our country to devastating enemy attack?" After a few minutes of silence, Ben continued, "You, my friend, are not answering my question." Ben sat down at his desk and looked across at Steve.

After more silence, Steve responded slowly. "I don't know Ben. I understand the predicament you are describing. I also understand that many young pilots have been killed, because you failed to take into account how the characteristics of each operating altimeter would cause planes to swerve out of control for a few seconds, enough time to often result in death.

"But what grabs me is the fact that even though you know about the problem and are re-designing the wing to account for it now, are still allowing the earlier models with the dangerous slats to continue flying. I am having a hard time reconciling the issue here, my friend. But of course I have to, don't I? At some point soon, I must write a report that either identifies the correct reason for the crashes or exonerates the Air Force and our company of any responsibility for the death of these young men." Steve continued. "So what would you do?"

"Don't ask me Steve. Your job and the future of the company are both at stake here. And if the company goes down, several thousand of us will go down with it. You don't expect an unbiased answer from me I hope." After a short time, Steve stood up, put on his coat and turned to go out.

"No, I guess I don't. But I wish I could find someone

who would offer one."

"You have been given an impossible job, Steve, one with which no one can help you. All the advice and suggestions in the world won't change the inevitable. The fact is that you, and only you, can make the final decision. I don't envy you in the least. I think you have all the facts, old buddy, now let's see what you do with them."

Steve nodded as he walked out the door. He smiled a very weak smile at Ben's secretary, Bev, and headed out the door to his car.

CHAPTER TWENTY-THREE

Steve drove into the parking lot of his favorite IHOP restaurant in hopes of grabbing a quick afternoon snack before getting home.

As he walked up to the front door he was aware of someone running after him. He turned to see a very attractive blonde woman, who he estimated to be in her late twenties, frantically waving at him.

"Mr. Pritchard. Please wait. I want to talk with you." Steve stopped and held the door open as she ran up to him out of breath. "Could I please have a word with you. It is about your search for the causes of the F-87 crashes?" Steve looked around to see if anyone was close enough to hear.

"Um, okay let's go sit in an empty corner of the restaurant so we can talk." He noticed that she had a particularly trim figure, as she smiled and walked ahead of him into the restaurant.

He asked, "Can I buy you a cup of coffee, or something?" They both sat down in a deserted corner of the restaurant.

As she sat down, she smiled and shook her head, pulling her blond hair back from her face. As he picked up the menu and opened it, he asked, "What can I do for you? Please forgive me but I haven't had lunch today." She smiled and nodded

"No problems Mr. Pritchard. Please go ahead and eat. I have some things to discuss with you that I hope won't disturb your lunch." She had a radiant smile to go with her beautiful hair and well-proportioned body. "I've been following you for some time hoping to get a chance to talk with you in private." Steve had a hard time selecting his lunch and listening to her at the same time.

"You see I'm a widow of a F-87 accident. My husband, Captain Bill Jackson, was killed in a crash of the fighter in very suspicious circumstances. The Air Force ruled it, 'pilot error,' but Bill was too experienced a pilot to have flown his plane directly into the ground as he was trying to land."

Steve ordered his lunch. "Yes, go on."

"Well, several other widows that I've met have hired an attorney and are pursuing our legal options in the situation." The waitress brought Steve his lunch.

"Could I offer you one of my French fries or something? I hate eating alone."

"No thank you." Steve noticed what beautiful teeth she had. "So you were telling me about a group of F-87 widows who want to sue the Air Force." He took a bite out of his hamburger as ketchup dripped down his shirt.

She smiled and reached over to wipe the ketchup off his shirt. "No, of course we can't sue the Air Force, as you know. But there's a possibility of suing an Air Force supplier who builds a faulty product." Steve almost choked on his mouth full of fries. "However, we have one major problem."

"I think you have several problems, but don't let me stop you." Steve gulped down his coke.

Her smile overcame his desire to laugh at her as she

ignored his lame attempt at humor. "Our problem, Mr. Pritchard, is that we don't know exactly what causes the planes to crash. Without that knowledge, a fair settlement in court is virtually impossible, as you can see." She tossed her long hair out of her eyes again. "I'm sure that you can now know why I'm here to talk with you."

Steve ate the remnants of his sandwich and stared at her for a few minutes as she looked down at the table.

"I know I shouldn't be sitting here asking for your help, but I had no choice. We've tried everything, but no one has been able to help us. They all say that you, Major Pritchard, are the only person in the world who knows the answer to our problem. There are many of us who are counting on your help."

Steve felt the urge to pick his teeth, but knew that was not appropriate in front of a woman. He wiped his mouth with his napkin.

"So let me get this straight. You want me to tell you the cause of the F-87 flaws so that you can sue my company and maybe put us out of business."

There were tears in her eyes as she looked up at him.

"I hate to put it that way, but, yes, I guess you could say that." She reached for a Kleenex in her purse but couldn't find one. Steve reached into his pocket and offered her a clean handkerchief. She smiled a thank-you and wiped her eyes. "There is much more to this than your company, Mr. Pritchard. The lives of hundreds of pilots are at stake here. I am sure you understand that by now." She looked up at him from behind his handkerchief.

Steve said, "You may call me Steve."

She smiled again through her tears. "Thank you Steve." She put her head in her hands as she stared down at the table, blowing her nose in his handkerchief.

"Why do you think I have the answer to your question?"

Steve reached over and raised her head up with his hand so she could look at him with tears in her eyes. She smiled weakly.

"I pray that you do, because you are our last hope." She paused to wipe her eyes. "Our lawyer tells us that he will not pursue this case unless you can give us reason for these accidents. And I haven't even mentioned our children, the boys and girls who no longer have fathers. How many more of our children must carry their fathers to their graves before something is done to stop it?" She raised her head, threw her shoulders back and stared straight into his face. This motion seemed to emphasize her figure

"Well, maybe my report will tell you everything you need to know." Steve reached across the table for his bill.

"And maybe it won't. We all know the strain you are under, Steve. You will be reluctant to tell the whole truth for reasons that are obvious to all of us. If your report tries to whitewash the issue, there are many of us who will suffer, even more than have so far." Her bright blue eyes stared at him intently as she handed his handkerchief back to him.

Steve reached into his pocket, pulled out a few bills and set them down on the table for a tip. He then swung his legs around and sat up from the table. Reaching over to help her up he said, "So what more do you want now?"

"Are you willing to help us?" That beautiful smile returned on her face as her hair fell down around her mouth. She brushed it back.

Changing the subject, he asked as they walked together to the cash register. "By the way, what's your name?"

"What bad manners I have. My name is Yvonne Jackson, and I live in Orange County, just southeast of here. Please forgive me." She took his arm and smiled at him.

"As you know, Mrs. Jackson, the information you are requesting is top secret, and I would get into serious trouble if I told you even if I did know."

She squeezed his arm with an affectionate squeeze rubbing it against her breast and put her head on his shoulder. She suddenly stopped and turned toward him. "I have an idea. If you'll tell me the reason for my husband's death, I agree not to use the information until you've published your report." She stepped back and looked at him with a smile. "Then it'll be common knowledge, you won't be in trouble, but we'll be able to prepare our case." She put her arm in his again.

"Hmm, well maybe it might be okay." She moved in closer to his body. "Let me say that the problem lies with the wing slats. There is something wrong with the deployment mechanism." They stopped and turned to look at each other. "The altimeters that activate the deployment mechanisms cannot operate in exact sequence, so the planes' wings have different levels of lift for a few seconds causing the plane to rotate. That's about it in a nutshell."

She stared at the pavement as they walked toward their cars. "I'm not sure I understand this technical stuff, but I think our lawyer will." They stopped, and she looked at him.

"Thank you Steve. The wives and children of the brave pilots who have died all thank you and wish we could repay you somehow." She smiled again. "But I guess this will have to do." She reached up and gave him a long kiss on the mouth. She then turn and ran off toward her car, got in and drove off. Steve stood there watching her drive north along Sepulveda.

"Hey wait a minute. Orange County is south he shouted." But she couldn't hear him. "Oh well Maybe her lawyer works in El Segundo or Santa Monica." Steve got in his car and drove home.

CHAPTER TWENTY-FOUR

As Steve walked through his front door, all his family including his dog came running up to greet him. "Its great to see everybody." He gave each one a big hug and kiss. He tossed his things on the sofa and undid his tie. "So what's been happening while I've been gone?"

"Nothing much here, Love. The important question is what's been happening with you?" Ellen put here arm though his and walked with him into the kitchen. "Let's go sit on the patio with our drinks, and you can tell me all about it."

"Sounds good to me," he said as he poured his gin and tonic. "I need to kick back and relax. And what's for dinner? I had a late hamburger but that didn't kill my appetite." He shared with his family all he could without divulging any secrets. After some minutes of sitting by himself, Ellen called the family into dinner.

After dinner, the two of them went back onto the patio next to the swimming pool and sat back to watch the sun set over the Pacific. Steve took a sip from his steaming coffee mug. "I wish all of life were as simple as sitting out here on this beautiful patio and watching the sunset." Ellen smiled and reached over to pat him on the arm. "Unfortunately, the more you know, the more complicated it gets," Steve mumbled. Neither spoke for a few minutes.

"So are you going to tell me the whole story, including the part about how you got lipstick on your lower lip?" Her smile was not quite as loving as it had been a few minutes before.

Steve had wiped his mouth during dinner but not well enough to remove the evidence. He pulled out his handkerchief, rubbed his lips and looked down at it. "Oh that."

"And I have to say, that's a very exotic perfume on your handkerchief. I could smell it when you walked into the room."

He folded up his handkerchief and put it back in his pocket. With all of the calmness he could muster, he replied, "Of course my dear. Its not what you think though."

"Well I'd really like to hear what caused your clothes to get permeated with lipstick and perfume. This may well be a good story, one I will probably want to remember," she replied with a sarcastic smile.

"As I said dear, it's not what you imagine. Otherwise I would have taken more care to destroy the evidence, don't you think?" He was proud of his retort. "Anyway, I need to start back where I had left off in our last discussion."

"Yes dear. Please do."

After over an hour and some intense technical information, he sat back with a third, maybe fourth, cup of coffee. "Anyway, the technical part fell into place rather easily once Charlie made her comment about the altimeter. My problem now, and the most serious of all concerns about this issue, is do I tell it like it is? Or do I whitewash it and let the accidents keep piling up until the new models are operational, and the original version with the movable wing slats gets replaced?"

"So tell me again how this woman that you met today

with the strong perfume fit into this?"

"Well as I said, her husband was killed in a crash of the Γ-87 several months ago, and she and some friends want to sue my company for building a faulty product."

"So she asked you to give her the details of the planes' failures so they would have a good case. Don't you think that's a little risky, giving a perfect stranger, no matter how attractive, classified information?

"But let me guess. She was beautiful, stood close to you, cried a lot and used your handkerchief to wipe her eyes, tricks women have been using for thousands of years. I'm surprised you fell for it. But I guess all men are alike. Can't resist a beautiful woman." Ellen shook her head in disbelief. "Let's hope that Western Aviation doesn't find out about your little tryst."

"It was not a tryst! I only helped a widow and her friends with their lawsuit. I don't see how that will be a problem." Steve continued, "However, I can see where it might be embarrassing to my company."

Ellen just shook her head again. "Your story raises some important questions about your judgment, questions that I have never considered before." She started to say more but thought better of it. She sat silently looking at him with an intensity that Steve had not seen before.

"Beyond all of that, I have to make an important decision and make it soon. Our future, the future of my company and the safety of our country as well as the lives of many airmen will depend on what I do next." Steve said as he put his head in his hands.

"May I offer my opinion?" Ellen asked as she got up and began walking around the patio. Steve knew pacing was not a good sign. "Besides all this technical gobble-dygook, the one thing that sticks with me the most, and correct me if I misunderstood you, was that you said that

118

if you told the truth, you would lose your job. Furthermore your company would see to it that you would never work in the aerospace business again." Her smile disappeared, and her stare intensified.

"You couldn't work at Lockheed, Hughes, Douglas, Rocketdyne, McDonnell, Aerojet, Boeing or any of their suppliers. That's the only business you know. If you took any other job, your salary would be miniscule, even if you could get a job." She was getting worked up. "We would lose this beautiful home." She threw her arms out and swung around. "In short we would lose everything we have worked for."

"You could go back teaching math in high school." He knew it was the wrong thing to say as soon as he said it, but it was too late.

"What do you mean I could go to work? I haven't taught in fifteen years." Now she was almost screaming. "That is not an option." She glared at him with an intensity he had never seen before. She walked to the other end of the pool with her hands on her hips. She finally returned and sat down staring at him. "No you don't have a big decision to make. It is simple. Do exactly what I, your company and the Air Force want you to do, and learn to live with it." Ellen got up and walked briskly to the patio doors. She turned back to him.

"And let me be clear. You left out one important consideration, our marriage and your children. We'll all be gone if you make the wrong choice!" She paused, looked him straight in the eyes and mumbled almost inaudibly, "Sometimes this being a mother and a wife isn't all it's cracked up to be." She turned and marched up to their bedroom.

Steve sat staring out at the ocean. After some time, he turned and picked up the day's Los Angeles Times. He opened up to the front page with his mind on his problems and not on the news. Then he saw the headline and sat up with a start.

Pilot Killed in Airplane Crash At El Toro

Yesterday an Air Force F-87 crashed on a landing approach to El Toro Marine Base in Orange County. Eyewitnesses said that the fighter was making what appeared to be a routine approach to the airstrip when it suddenly rotated to the left and crashed bursting into flame. The pilot had no chance to eject and was killed instantly. His identity was withheld pending notification of next of kin.

"My God. Another one!" Steve gasped as he again stared out at the ocean. "If I'd spoken up sooner, maybe he'd be alive today. I've got make a decision pretty soon or I'll have more blood on my hands," he thought. He picked the paper up again hoping to see better news. When he read to the bottom of the first page, he jumped again.

FBI warning to be on the lookout for a Soviet Spy.

The FBI put out a warning today that a notorious Soviet spy is in the Los Angeles area and is very dangerous. She is an expert in obtaining classified information and all citizens are urged to contact the authorities if she is spotted.

Her description is as follows: In her late twenties, long blond hair, trim figure and blue eyes, about five feet four inches tall. She specializes in using her beauty to obtain classified information about weapons systems from men who work in the aerospace business.

"Oh shit!" Steve shouted and rose up and threw the paper down. Now I'm in real trouble. I've got to talk with someone I can trust. At least tomorrow is Saturday." He picked up the phone.

"Hello Steve. What's up?"

"High Charlie. I've got to talk with you. Could you fly down to LAX tomorrow morning? I'll meet you in the baggage claim area at about 10:00."

"Sure Steve. What's going on? You sound terrible."

"Yeah, I've probably had too much to drink. I'll tell you more tomorrow morning." Steve hung up the phone and stared up at the night sky. A shiver ran down his back as he poured himself another drink.

CHAPTER TWENTY-FIVE

Captain Pritchard climbed into the cockpit of his Mustang and fastened his seatbelt. The engine was idling gently with the signature purr of the Rolls-Royce Merlin. He checked all of the controls and instruments and finally signaled to the ground crew to remove the wheel chocks so he could taxi out onto the runway. He had noticed that someone in his ground crew had painted the ninth and tenth swastikas on the fuselage just under the cockpit. He was now a double ace and he didn't care who knew it. He reached back and slid the cockpit canopy forward as he waved goodbye to his ground crew. The oil pressure was in its acceptable range and the engine temperature was rising slowly into its normal range. He had made the fuel mixture a little richer than normal as was customary in preparation for warm up and take off.

One of his crew had climbed up onto the left wing to signal him as he taxied out onto the end of the runway. The Mustang was the last "tail dragger" that made it difficult for the pilot to see over the nose when taxiing. Consequently, a ground crewman who had good visibility was designated to lie on his stomach on the wing and give the pilot directions. Steve shoved the throttle forward as the crewman slid off the wing onto the tarmac. The Merlin growled, as anxious as he was to be airborne.

After a routine takeoff, he looked down at the quickly disappearing green English countryside. He raised the landing gear and closed the flaps while climbing through the first layer of clouds and into the bright morning sunshine that was rare in England at this time of year. He looked around for his wingmen and saw nothing but clear sky. "That's strange," he mumbled. "I guess they're coming up behind me." He pointed the nose of his fighter higher to increase his rate of climb. He glanced down at his altimeter and saw it climb through 15,000 feet. He put on his oxygen mask, leaned out the mixture to a cruising level and set his course for the Dutch coast to rendezvous with the B-17's he was escorting over Germany.

What a beautiful day he thought. He turned and glanced to his right toward the French coast, when he saw them; three specks headed toward him at about 20,000 feet. "Those can't be friends. I'd better prepare for the worst," he mumbled to himself.

The problem with identifying the German Messerschmitt ME-109 was that they looked very much like his Mustang when they were headed directly toward you. Whoever designed the Mustang employed their clipped wings and water-cooled engine to make the best fighter plane ever designed, the P-51 Mustang. Steve stared at the three dots, as they got bigger. He slowly banked right into them and removed the safety from the firing button that controlled his six .50 caliber machine guns just in case.

He slowly pushed the throttle forward watching his airspeed as he had done so many times. He was now on a collision course with the lead plane closing at perhaps eight hundred miles an hour. Suddenly the lead plane showed flashes of light coming from around the engine and on its wings. Only the ME-109 had its guns mounted around the engine with cannon in the wings, so there was no doubt what Steve was facing. He opened up with his six .50 caliber machine guns in answer as the Germans split in three directions as quickly and smoothly as ballet dancers.

Steve turned hard right to get behind one of them and pulled up behind as one of the German wingmen moved into his sight. He carefully lined up on him with just a little lead and pulled his trigger. His Mustang erupted with a blast of fire from its .50 caliber guns as he watched his tracers stream toward the now sharply turning ME-109. His enemies had tried this maneuver on him before without luck. He turned more sharply to keep his tracers streaming into the enemy, and he was scoring hits.

At least that was what he thought he saw. But nothing happened. The German kept flying through his stream of tracers as his slugs tore through the fuselage, the engine and then the wings, but nothing happened. The German kept flying without damage until he finally turned out of Steve's field of vision.

Steve sat dumbstruck watching his enemy disappear around behind him. "What the hell happened?" He had never fired at such an easy set up shot and had the plane survive. "I can't believe this," he shouted to himself in frustration.

As he leveled off looking around for another target, he suddenly saw two of the 109s maneuver alongside him, one on each side. He looked in horror as he saw the plane on his left and read the numbers on its fuselage. "My God. That's the plane I shot down two days ago. I remember its number," he shouted at his control panel. He looked into the cockpit and saw the pilot smiling at him. The German saluted him and turned off. Steve turned to look at the plane on his right and read its number. "Christ! It's Otto Kittel, one of Germany's top aces with over a hundred kills. He's smiling at me. What have I got here?" The German peeled off to his right leaving Steve flying alone along the French coast.

Suddenly a long burst of 20 mm tracers and machine gun fire erupted from behind his plane. Steve rotated down and to the left, a maneuver that usually left his pursuers empty-handed, but not this time. Whoever was on his six was a better pilot than he thought, and nothing Steve did could shake him.

Bullets streamed passed and into his wings and engine. He could hear them bounce off the armor behind his pilot's seat. Thank God for the armor, he thought, but his plane was coming apart. No matter what maneuver he tied, it was no use.

Now metal peeled off the wings, oil streamed out of the engine, and fire flamed out of the wings as the propeller slowed to a stop. The nose of his Mustang now dropped as he headed out of control at a very high speed toward the French countryside. He was about to pay for all those Germans he had killed. He pulled back on the stick. Nothing happened. He tried to scream. Nothing came out. He tried to open the canopy, but it was stuck closed. The ground got closer and closer. He closed his eyes in anticipation of the worst. "So this is what it feels like to die."

He suddenly awoke in terror and threw off the covers as his feet slammed onto the floor.

"My God what a dream!" He rested his head in his hands for a moment then turned to look over at Ellen who was snoring lightly next to him. He looked at the clock at the bedside. It read 2:15.

"I couldn't save myself no matter what I did and was at the mercy of my enemies," he thought to himself as he tried to make sense of it all. I haven't had a dream like that since

I left England. He stumbled into the bathroom and wiped the sweat from his face.

Later that morning walking through the LAX terminal Charlie asked, "Are you feeling better?" Steve nodded, picked up Charlie's bag and took her by the arm as they walked briskly toward the hourly parking lot. "Slow down a bit, will you. My legs aren't as long as yours."

"Oh, sorry."

"So where are we headed?"

Steve smiled. "I'm going to show you the place I always go when things get tough. Now into the car with you." He helped her in, closed the door and went around to the driver's side. "The plot has thickened since the last time we talked. But before we get into that, remind me later to tell you about the nightmare I had last night. It was the worst dream I've had since I was a kid. However, let's talk about my latest troubles first."

"I assumed that there was something new going on after our brief conversation last night." Charlie looked over at him but said nothing more for a while. "So, we're headed south. You're not taking me home with you I hope."

Steve laughed. "No Charlie. There are other places south of the airport besides Palos Verdes." He turned toward her. "You wondered how I knew so much about sailboats. Now you are going to find out." When they reached Long Beach, he turned southeast continuing down the Pacific Coast Highway soon crossing into Orange County.

"Have you ever been to Newport Beach?"

"Umm, I think I was here once some years ago after we beat USC in a football game; some of us had dinner at that big restaurant over there I think." Steve turned into a gated parking lot next to a series of docks protruding out into Newport Harbor. The docks were filled with a number

126

of large, unmanned, moored sail and powerboats. "Wow. Don't tell me that you have a boat here."

Steve smiled and looked down at her legs. "I forgot to tell you to wear tennis shoes, although I think there are a pair of my wife's on board. But I guess you are going to have to struggle with that skirt. No wait. My wife has a pair of shorts on board too, but you'll need to wrap them twice around that tiny waist of yours." Charlie looked over and grinned at him.

Steve opened the trunk and pulled out a large ice chest. "Let's see if we can find a boat with the right name on it." He gestured out across the sea of boats bobbing in the soft breeze. For the first time she noticed that he had on boat shoes and sailing slacks. He pulled a baseball cap out of the car emblazed with the word "Dodgers" written in blue across the front and pulled it down over his forehead. "Let's go." He opened the gate and helped her down the steep ramp onto the floating dock and out to a boat moored near the end of the dock in a windward slip. "If it says 'Polaris' on the stern, this is it."

"Wow, what are we looking at?" She stood staring out at a beautifully clean and well-kept sloop, with the sails stowed perfectly in blue storage bags and the wooden trim around the cabin well oiled.

"That, my dear, is a 43 foot Catalina sloop, fully rigged and ready to set sail. It is as long a boat as can be sailed by one person, and only then in relatively light winds, which is about all we have down here in Southern California."

Charlie noticed that this was the first time he had called her dear. "I'm impressed," she responded.

"I am not sure that we're actually going to set the sails today, but let me fire up this old diesel and motor out to see if we have any wind." He opened the hatch door and tossed the ice chest below. "Se if you can find any clothes and shoes that fit. Meanwhile, we'll get underway.

"Do you need any help up there?"

"No I don't. And by the way, why don't you stay below until we reach the outer channel buoys. I have lots of friends on these docks who know our phone number." Steve could hear a chuckle come from the forward berth.

Charlie could feel the light swell that indicated that they had motored out of the channel and into the Pacific. She stuck her head up and looked around. "Is it okay if I come out now? She smiled up at him and, not waiting for an answer slid onto the seat across from Steve.

"Cute outfit," he smiled.

"The next time you invite a woman sailing, you should provide her with the proper wearing apparel." She threw her sweater on her shoulders over her light blouse to keep off the ocean breeze as she rose and moved over to the bench next to Steve. "So what are we facing now?" She looked up at him.

"Funny you should ask. As my friend Ben said yesterday, only I can make this final decision." As the swells and the wind increased slightly, she snuggled in closer to him.

"You have told me about Ben before Steve, but are you sure he is your friend?"

Steve turned toward her. "Of course he's my friend. We've been friends since the war. Why wouldn't you think that he's my friend?" Steve replied with a little irritation in his voice. "Anyway, he was in on most of my discussion with the big boss yesterday and knows more about the problem than anyone else."

"Yet he told you nothing nor even gave you a hint about the problem, right?" Steve scowled at her. "Just asking," she replied softly.

"Okay, okay. So now let me bring you up to date on the latest. I got us out here so we wouldn't be overheard."

128

"Oh shucks. I thought you brought me out here for other reasons." She slipped her arm under his and leaned her head against his shoulder.

CHAPTER TWENTY-SIX

They were both quiet for a while as the breeze freshened slightly out of the northwest, blowing Charlie's brown hair back off of her shoulders. She stared west toward the horizon obviously lost in thought. "So you're going to lose any chance of employment plus your wife and maybe your children if you speak the truth. Is that about it?"

"Yes, that's about it." Steve still hadn't raised the sails. "Some choice isn't it? Oh, there are a couple of things I forgot to mention. Here is an article in yesterday's Times; read it please." Charlie took the paper from him and read the front page.

"Oh my God." She put her hand over her mouth, "Another one goes in and kills the pilot."

"Now I've got to show you the clincher. Read this other article about the Soviet spy." Charlie sat up in alarm. "Oh Jesus Christ, you didn't fall for this 'cute little spy' trick did you? When are you men going to learn?"

Steve just shook his head. "I know."

"God Steve. What have you done? Well I guess that relieves you of one of the problems. You don't have to worry about telling the Russians. They know already." She folded the paper and tossed it below.

"I hadn't thought about it that way, but yes you're undoubtedly right," Steve responded. Charlie folded her arms and stared out toward the horizon.

"You've got a problem here my friend. How can I help?" She reached over and gripped his arm. He switched on the autopilot, turned to look at her and took both of her hands in his.

"I guess just listen to me talk and offer any suggestions that might come to mind. In the meantime I'm going to break open two bottles of brew." Steve dropped down into the cabin and she heard two bottles pop open. "Here you go." He passed one up to her.

"How come the wheel is turning by itself?" She stared back at the wheel moving back and forth as the autopilot was trying to stay on course. "Oh, I get it. Never mind."

"My wife is no help. She has a vested interest in the outcome." Steve leaned back against the gunwale next to her and took a long sip on his cold beer. "It's not easy to accept that my company knew about the issue from near the beginning and has done nothing to pull the problem fighters out of service."

"But you're beginning to accept it because you're not naïve. It's obvious what motivated your company, the Air Force and now your wife. Everyone enjoys the status quo, no one likes whistle blowers, and you're just the latest version. Wait until you actually blow the whistle. Then you are really going to feel their rage." Steve nodded as he took another sip.

"Every time I read another article about a plane going in, I'll think that I could have prevented it. On the other hand, if the Russians initiate a bomber attack against us, and we have no fighters to throw up against them, how will I feel then?"

"Man, I'm glad this is your problem. But listen Steve,"

she said as she turned toward him. "Whatever you do, you'll have my support. I'll sign your report in concurrence whichever way you go." Steve put his arm around her as she put her head on his shoulder.

After a few minutes he said, "It is really a simple problem, it's the solution that's difficult. I do have to eat and I can't survive without a job for long." He turned to her. "Do you suppose that my status as a World War II hero will see me through this? No, I guess not.

"What does it mean to be a hero anyway? Let's back up even further. What is a hero in the first place, someone who takes a chance and comes out a winner? Some of those German pilots I shot down were just as brave and as skilled as I, maybe even more so. And yet I'm alive and a hero and they, if they survived my aerial gunnery at all, are probably struggling to heal their wounds and keep their families alive after the war.

"There is nothing heroic about being a good shot. I can kill a duck flying at fifty yards too. So what?" He emptied out his bottle. "Shooting down twelve Messerschmitts is not heroic, it's just plain luck coupled with a little skill. Now I'm going to need more than luck. What's that the famous football coach once said? I'd rather have a lucky player than a good one. He wouldn't want me though. How about another beer?"

"No thanks. But help yourself."

"But maybe the Germans are the lucky ones. I doubt if any of my opponents who survived the war has to deal with problems like this." Steve came up with another beer in his hands, but stood for a moment in the companionway looking aft toward the coast. "Which brings one to ask, how did I get into this anyway?" He looked over at her. "Didn't they teach you anything at Stanford? Damn it anyway." He slid in beside her.

He continued. "You know, I had a similar moral dilemma in the summer of 1944. Others pilots in my squadron were saying that we should machine gun enemy pilots who had bailed out and were parachuting to the ground over Germany. Their argument was that the enemy pilots who safely parachuted to the ground would survive, get another plane and try to kill us again.

"I tried it once. At least I started to. I flew toward a German pilot after he had parachuted out of his burning plane that I had bagged; I had him square in my sights, but I couldn't pull the trigger. I turned away and flew past him staring into his eyes as I passed.

"I will never forget the look on his face. He was just a kid, probably not yet twenty and would just as easily have killed me. I often wondered if he survived the war. If he did, he owes me a beer. I have never been sorry for what I did. War is just a matter of life and death, and as a fighter pilot you have the power to kill beneath your thumb. This is worse."

"Not to change the subject, but are you sure we should be out this far?" Charlie looked around at the empty sea.

"Yes, you're right. If we had the main up we could be riding these swells easier."

"That's not what I meant and you know it." She gave his arm a playful squeeze.

"There are no winners in this game of life are there? There are only different degrees of loser. No matter what decision I make, it'll be wrong." Steve slumped down. "Yes, you can be a winner for a while, but how many planes have I shot down lately? When I make this decision I will no longer be the great war hero, will I?"

"You've had too many beers, Steve. You had better be sure you can get us back to land."

"Yea, the harbor entrance is back there somewhere.

We've got to remember that the current along this coast is setting us south. It wouldn't do to get stuck out here over night with a beautiful girl on board. I have enough problems as it is." He grinned, put his arm around her waist and gave her a big squeeze. "Let's turn north to compensate for the drift. That mountain there off our starboard bow is on the Palos Verdes peninsula. I don't want to get too close. Nor do I want to end up in San Diego."

"Wherever starboard is and whatever you say skipper. My life is in your hands" She reached up and kissed him on the cheek as she pulled her sweater tighter over her shoulders.

Soon Steve added, "It is getting nippy out here. Maybe we should head home. Hang on. We will be taking swells on our broadside for a few seconds until we are headed to the east." He took the helm off autopilot and rotated the wheel all the way around to the right. "We're headed home, and if I can just find the harbor entrance buoys, we'll be okay."

"Swell. You really like to make a girl nervous don't you?" She craned her neck looking forward around the cabin to see if she could find the buoys herself. "By the way. You haven't told me about your bad dream last night." She looked at him with a motherly smile on her face. "I like interpreting dreams. Let's see if I can help." She put her head on his shoulder.

"I think it's pretty easy to interpret. One of the German pilots I shot down came back to haunt me." Steve told her the story of his dream with only small embellishments. "Somewhere in my subconscious I seem to feel guilty about the men I've killed. I've never felt guilty before. They were the enemy and it was them or me, wasn't it?" He turned to look at her. She kept her head on his shoulder.

"What gets me about the dream was that there was

nothing I could do to shoot them down or keep my plane from being shot-up. Everything was stacked against me. Sort of like my problem that we are trying to solve now, isn't it?" Neither spoke for a few minutes. "Maybe my subconscious self is trying to tell me something." Charlie slowly raised her head off of Steve's shoulder and looked into his eyes.

"Okay soldier, what do we have here? You think that there is an answer to what we're doing, a solution that will fit neatly into a logical package. What if there isn't? What if there's no answer to life's problems, only questions? She stared south along the California coast.

"You know the old saying that all of life's decisions have to be made with insufficient data. At Stanford we were taught to use complicated calculus equations to solve complex problems in aeronautical design, as I'm sure you were at UCLA. But can this problem be solved with calculus? I think not. We are left with the lessons we've learned growing up and, yes, in killing people along the way." Steve spotted the harbor entrance buoy but didn't want to interrupt her with the news.

"Umm. That's interesting." He looked up at the circling seagulls that indicated they were close to land.

"Don't say anything you don't mean," she smiled and squeezed his arm tighter. That was okay with him because he couldn't think of anything to say anyway. "And let's get this baby home before dark. There's no telling what will happen if we're stuck out here all night."

CHAPTER TWENTY-SEVEN

The sun was dropping low over the ocean as he drove up his driveway, but there were several more hours of daylight left. He noticed a strange car parked in front of his home, but Ellen's car was gone. He stepped out and walked around to head up to the front door when he noticed that two people had stepped out of the strange car and were walking up his front steps toward him. He stopped and, looking down at them, noticed that one was a handsome young man in his thirties walking with a limp and supported by a cane. The other was a beautiful woman several years younger who was helping the man navigate the steps leading up to their front door. As they got closer, Steve saw that the man had short-cropped blond hair and was indeed as handsome as he had first appeared. He waited for them to reach him.

"Major Pritchard?" the young man asked with a slight accent as they reached the porch.

"Yes, that's me."

"Good. I havf finally found you." He smiled as he switched his cane to his left hand and reached out his right hand. Steve responded and shook his hand firmly.

"Let me introduce us. My name is Hans Richter and

this is my vife Elsa." She smiled and nodded. "Ve came here from Germany."

"Well, your English is excellent. What can I do for you?"

"May ve come in and visit with you for a few minutes. Ve won't take much of your time."

"Sure. I guess. My wife and children are off doing something, probably shopping. But you're welcome to come in." He opened the front door and ushered them in. "Let's go out to the pool and sit. The day still has plenty of sun left in it." He noticed that Hans favored his right leg supporting it with his cane as he walked. "Can I get you a beer or a cup of tea?"

"No, thank you Sir." Steve was glad that they didn't want tea. He didn't know where Ellen kept the tea bags. They all sat and Hans and Elsa had big smiles on the faces.

"First of all Major, let me tell you how ve got here and why ve havf been looking for you. Ve arrived in Los Angeles yesterday, rented the car you see out there, rented a hotel room by the airport and came here to visit you. Tomorrow ve'll be driving north along the coast to see San Francisco and your redwood forest. This is the first vacation ve have had since the war. But it is more than a vacation. I have been searching for you since 1944, with no luck until today.

"You see Major, I am the Luftwaffe pilot that you shot down over Germany in the summer of '44, but you didn't shoot me in my parachute on the way down. I vas a lowly lieutenant then and was flying as the wingman to the German ace Captain Otto Kittel. You came down from behind and above us. You fired first at Otto's plane and it exploded in flames, then you turned your plane toward me and fired a short burst that destroyed my oil cooler. As I rolled to the right to get away from your attack, my engine froze

137

for lack of oil, and I rotated it onto its back, opened the canopy, unfastened my seat belt and fell out of the cockpit. Fortunately my chute opened, and I floated toward to what I thought would be a safe landing. Then I saw you turn around and head back toward me.

"I was terrified because I was helpless in the parachute as I saw your Mustang heading directly at me. I saw my life drifting away, but you did a miraculous thing. You suddenly turned away and didn't fire your guns. You flew close by me, raised your right hand in a salute and flew away." Hans stopped talking for a minute to see if Steve remembered and recognized him.

Steve was shocked at his story and its reference to Otto, the German pilot in his nightmare. He had never known the name of that particular pilot, so how could he have appeared in his dream? He had, not knowing who he was, killed him in a shoot out and then Otto returned in a dream years later. Wow! Something is strange here.

He looked over at Elsa and noticed that she had tears in her eyes on top of her smile.

"Yes, I remember the incident well. You were my eighth kill as I recall. Sorry for using a bad word."

"No problem Major. Ve in the Luftwaffe used the same vord."

"How did you find me? How did you even know who I was?

"Vell, let me finish my story. When you flew by I saw the markings on your plane's fuselage and tail and vowed never to forget them. Things got worse when I landed. The wind in my chute dragged me along the ground and into the side of a barn. I broke my right ankle. It was so badly smashed that I havf still not recovered its use. In fact, my doctors tell me that I will probably always havf a limp. However, I am alive because of you and will never forget that.

"They took me to a hospital in Frankfurt where I had good care and was treated vell, but ve were short on medicine. When the war ended I was still in the hospital recovering slowly. One of your army orthopedic surgeons took over my case and I did better. At least I could get around with a cane enough to marry my sweetheart Elsa here." He reached over and patted her on her knee.

"I finally found a job and vent to work in West Germany supporting the two of us, but always knowing that someday I would find you. I wrote your Air Force trying to find someone in your squadron that might know you, but without luck. Finally, a few months ago, someone wrote back that your squadron was having a reunion in New Orleans last week so ve came over hoping that you would be there."

"Oh my. I forgot about it and missed the reunion."

"Ya you did. Ve were there, and as a former enemy, I vas treated very well. Everyone wanted to buy me a drink as ve talked over mutual battles. They voted me in as an honorary member of your squadron and invited me to your next reunion in Miami. They even invited me to give one of the keynote addresses. I finally found someone who knew you and gave us your address. Ve came straight here from New Orleans and that is pretty much the end of my story, except for two things. First of all I want to thank you for giving me my life."

Elsa then jumped up and came over to Steve. "Ja, Major. I don't speak English so vell as Hans does, but I havf vaited to give you this big hug und danke und a kiss of mine own." Steve was startled to get a big hug and kiss from such a pretty young wife. He smiled and mumbled something incoherently.

"Now our big news is that Elsa is finally pregnant. Ve

have been trying for years, and now she presented me with the news just before we left. Ve consider you to be the grandfather, and, if it is a boy, ve will name him Steve, and if it a girl her name vill be Stephanie."

Steve opened his mouth but couldn't think of anything to say. He just smiled and finally said, "Thank you." Now tears were welling up in his eyes. He pulled out his handkerchief and finally was able to say, "But you haven't told me the second reason you came from the other side of the world to visit me."

"This is one that has kept me awake at night. That is, vhy did you do it? Vhy didn't you kill me, your sworn enemy, when you had a chance? You first saved my life and then saluted me as if you were respecting me, even though you didn't even know me.

After a few minutes he continued, "You and I lost many friends in the var Major, but ve both survived although I havf a sore ankle to show for it. It just doesn't make sense to me." Hans stopped talking and stared at Steve.

Steve looked down at the floor and then back at Hans.

"I'm sorry Hans, but I have no quick answer to your question and have wondered the same thing myself. There seems to be some innate nature in human beings that tends to dictate their behavior. I didn't have time to stop and think about what to do when you were in my gun sight. I just saw another human being dangling at the end of a parachute cord, unable to defend himself.

It's rather like helping a beggar asking for money for food. If you stopped to think about it, you could convince yourself that he would probably spend whatever you gave him on liquor or cigarettes. But your immediate reaction is to give him a couple of quarters. So what if he spends it on booze? I have found that when I fail to help someone in need, that I spend the rest of the night worrying that I didn't do the right thing.

"Maybe that's what I knew I would be doing if I had killed you that day. How would I sleep for the rest of my life? How could I explain to my kids and grandkids that I shot a helpless enemy trying to save his own life? As they say, war is hell. But the toughest part of war is the need to make the decision to kill someone else. I'm sure that you've faced the same decision Hans. Would you really have pulled the trigger on me under similar circumstances?" Hans stared down at the floor.

"I honestly don't know, Major" Hans smiled.

"But that's a decision that neither of us will have to make now. We can spend the rest of our lives wondering why without having to answer that question. Now, however, its time to have a beer and talk about the future and not the past." Steve heard a car pull up into their driveway as he opened three beers in the kitchen.

Steve introduced Ellen, Matt, Jennifer, and Carolyn. Then he explained what the two Germans were doing there, and everyone exchanged helloes before the kids went off to do their homework. Hans and Elsa invited Steve and Ellen to dinner, saying that they wouldn't take no for an answer. Ellen got a baby sitter quickly and they went out to the best restaurant in Long Beach.

"That was a very interesting couple you had here this afternoon." Ellen turned over in their bed and looked at Steve. "It's not every day that someone you once tried to kill drops by to thank you. I don't remember that you ever told me that story, Steve. Had you?"

"Probably not. I have never been quite sure whether to be proud of it or ashamed of it. Now that I've met Hans and his wife, I feel that I can brag about it. I'm glad that you took a picture of us. I think I'll have it enlarged and set on the piano. People need to see that I made at least one correct decision in my life. Now I think I'll go to sleep."

"Helen called today. She saw you motoring alone out of the bay early this afternoon and didn't return for several hours. Did you get the sails up?"

Steve opened his eyes. "No, I just wanted to motor around and think a while. Raising the mainsail alone on a forty-three foot sloop is no easy task, as you know." He waited for Ellen's reply.

"That's what I thought you were up to. Good night, Dear."

"Good night, Honey"

CHAPTER TWENTY-EIGHT

It was a bright Sunday morning and Steve was sitting on a bench at the edge of a beautiful city park not far from his home. It was a typical Southern California day, rather cool in the morning with the prospects of higher temperatures as the day wore on. A brisk breeze was blowing off of the ocean from the southwest. Steve looked up at the high fog bank that was rapidly dissipating and letting the morning sun begin to break through.

A pad of yellow paper rested on his lap and he fingered a pen that he had taken out of his pocket. He looked down at what he had written. "In the matter of the unexplained crashes of the F-87 Leopard fighter plane." He put that down twenty minutes ago and then stopped. He has written nothing since.

"Pardon me Sir, but could I bother you for a little change, so that I could buy lunch? I haven't eaten in two days?" Steve looked up at a young man sporting a several days old beard and wearing clothes that he had apparently been in for two weeks.

"Sure. A couple of bucks should get you a hamburger." Steve reached into his wallet and pulled out two crisp one-dollar bills and handed them to the stranger.

"Thank you Sir. I'm much obliged." He turned to walk away.

"Pardon me young man, but may I ask why are you begging rather than searching for a job?" Steve was immediately sorry he asked a question that was none of his business.

The young man turned back to face him. "I guess I don't mind telling you ... if I can sit down? Begging takes lots of standing." Steve scooted over to give him room on the bench.

"First of all it's Sunday and no one hires on Sundays even if they have a job. But mostly, its pretty hard getting a job when you are homeless. ... I wasn't always homeless... just a few months ago I had a great job as a draftsman in a big company right here in Long Beach. But, they decided to close up the plant and move its operation to Texas. ... Taxes are lower there, as are wages. ... "They wouldn't move Long Beach employees to Texas; they wanted all new ones. So all of us lost our work. Since I have no job, I couldn't pay my mortgage .... I lost my home, too, although I had paid my car off.

"You realize when an entire plant shuts down, finding another job is even harder because several hundred of us are all competing for the same few jobs that might be available! Guess the bigwigs making the decisions never think about that, do they?" he asked, looking quizzically at Steve.

"And there are no facilities in this part of the world to house those of us who are homeless even if it's 'cause we're jobless! Apparently, folks all think that we did something wrong to lose our jobs and homes... So I sleep in my car and beg for food.

"You don't by any chance know if anyone is hiring do you?" Again, the man looked at Steve.

"As a matter of fact, maybe I do. Here's my card. Notice the address. Go there after getting cleaned up, and ask for Jim Osborn, the personnel director. Show him my card and tell him that I recommended you. If he has anything, I am sure that he will give it to you."

The young man jumped up and looking down at the card said, "Oh thank you! I will indeed follow up on this." He turned and walked away briskly.

Steve looked back down at his yellow pad. "Okay, I've gotten the first sentence written. Now what do I say?" He looked back up at the young man receding in the distance. "So that's what happens when a plant closes," he said in a soft voice. "Maybe I need to pay attention."

He folded up his yellow pad, stood up and began to wander aimlessly across the park. "I haven't had anyone to talk to about this since I put Charlie on the plane back to San Jose yesterday," he said to himself.

He stopped to watch a group of small boys playing baseball. "Boy I was a star shortstop in my day. What ever happened to my day?" Just then the batter hit a sharp ground ball to the shortstop. He waited for it to arrive and then let it roll between his legs and out into left field. "I did my share of that, too," he mused as he walked on.

He stopped at another bench, sat down, opened his tablet and put his pen to it, ready to write.

"'Guess the bigwigs making the decisions never think about that, do they?'" echoed in Steve's mind and the man's gray eyes reappeared in Steve's vision.

"All the reports prepared by the Air Force concluded that the crash was caused by pilot error," Steve thought again. He stared at his tablet, then stood up, closed it and started walking again. "My second sentence at this rate is going to take a while," he said to a squirrel that sat quietly looking up at him hoping for a handout..

The sound of a commercial airliner in a landing pattern for the Long Beach airport interrupted his tangled thinking. Its flaps were down and its landing gear was dropping into position. He stared after it until it disappeared behind some buildings at the end of the runway. He continued staring into the empty sky for a few minutes and then he walked up to a park bench, sat down, opened his notebook and began writing.

CHAPTER TWENTY-NINE

It was another bright, sunny, slightly smoggy Southern California afternoon when Steve walked into the hotel and picked up the phone in the lobby. He asked the operator to connect him to Charlene Collins' room. The phone rang and a familiar voice answered, "Hello."

"Ah, I caught you," Steve sounded relieved.

"Oh, hi Steve. What's up?"

"I'm down in the lobby with a rough draft of our report and a typed copy of the front page for you to sign. May I come up?"

"Sure. Come on up. I'm in room 517."

"I'm off" Steve answered as he hung up and headed for the elevator taking big strides.

Steve was shocked when Charlie opened the door with a big smile on her face. It wasn't the smile that caught his attention; it was how she was dressed and how her hair was done up. She was wearing a low cut, tight fitting blouse over short tight skirt. Her hair, although fairly short cut, was no longer tied on the back of her head. It was typical for professional women of the day to look as un-sexual as possible and Charlie had been no exception. But today she looked like a teen-age girl headed for the Friday night school dance. "Did she know I was coming?" Steve thought.

"Well --- good afternoon." Steve managed a stutter. "May I come in?"

"Of course silly." Charlie stepped back to let Steve into her room. As Steve passed close by her body he noticed that same perfume she always wore and that drove him crazy. But today it seemed more intense. "Please grab a chair," she motioned to a chair in the corner.

Charlie closed the door behind them and walked over to the just-made-up queen sized bed. She stacked up both pillows at the head and pulled her legs back under her as she stretched out on the bed with her back to the pillows. It made her look more beautiful than she probably was. She smiled at him. "So, did you drive all the way to smoggy downtown L.A. just to see me?"

Steve gathered his breath, "Yea. But first of all I was worried that you had gone back to Palo Alto. He then reached into his briefcase, opened it and pulled out a sheet of paper to hand to her. "It's the title page of our final report, which we both need to sign. You've told me that you'd agree with whatever I wrote, so here it is." He wasn't quite sure that he should be sitting in her hotel room.

Charlie took the sheet from him, glanced down at it and saw her typed name under "Co-Author." She reached over to the bedside stand, pulled out a pen and signed the document. She handed it back to him and asked, "So, now that I've signed it, tell me what I just signed."

Steve noticed her beautiful red fingernails. "Yea, I guess I owe you that, don't I?" He tried his best not to look at her curled up on her bed. It was almost more than he could take. "This just isn't like her," he thought.

He stumbled on. "I have more work to do on it yet, but it pretty much says that the F-87 has a faulty design that

148

has caused the death of many Air Force pilots." Steve tried to look away from her but couldn't take his eyes off her for long.

"I ... I mean we ... get into the design of the slats without pinning blame on anyone specifically. I thought that it was not necessary to mention names, because it was obvious who had designed the plane. We concluded that all of the planes should be pulled out of service until the problem is fixed."

Steve wondered if Charlie was listening as she stared intently back at him. He knew that she was fond of him, but today she had a look about her that said she was not going to be denied.

"When I leave here, I'll go back home and stay up as long as necessary to finish it up. Louise, my secretary, has been alerted that she will get it tomorrow before noon, so I can present the final typed version to Mr. Stern before he goes home tomorrow. She's a great typist and will do a top-notch job."

Charlie nodded slowly. Neither could think of what to say next.

"So I guess that this marks the end of our friendship. You go your way and I'll go mine until another project comes along." She paused, looking quizzically at Steve to see his reaction to her remark. He appeared calm but felt far from calm inside.

He was staring down at the floor, as was his custom when he was confused. He looked up. "Not exactly. We'll always be friends, won't we? But I guess you're right," he stammered. "There's lots I could say, maybe lots I should say. But none of it would be appropriate under the circumstances, so I think I had better go now." He started to rise out of his chair.

"No you don't, Buster." Charlie jumped off the bed,

and, ran over to where he was sitting and shoved Steve back down in his chair with her hands firmly pushing down on his shoulders "You don't get away that easily. Don't even think about leaving until I say you can." Steve was startled with her directness. He couldn't move.

She began to walk around the room. "You came into my life like a whirlwind, waltzed me up and down the west coast, used me as a sounding board, took me out to dinner and lunch at the officer's club, took me out on your sailboat and now you're going to say goodbye, just like that!" Charlie stopped at the window and looked down through the L.A. smog at the street below..

After a minute she looked westward toward the Pacific, barely discernible above the layer of smog. "So this is what love brings you. My mother warned me about falling in love. 'It is fraught with dangers and hard times,' she said. She never told me that I was going to end up in my hotel room saying goodbye to the man I love. Now I'm supposed to be satisfied that I'll never see that man again."

She turned to look directly at him. "Yes, you idiot, I've fallen madly in love with you. And yes, I suspect that you know it. You may be an engineer, but you're no fool." Charlie smiled at her little joke, as Steve looked up into her eyes noticing that she suddenly looked ten years more mature than her age. He was taken with her self-confidence.

"I hate it when women get in touch with their feelings and are not afraid to share them," Steve thought to himself.

She sat in a chair across the room before continuing, "You are not responding, so I have no option but to finally tell you, thank you for the gift of love these past few months. I only wish that you could have accepted and returned the unconditional love that I have offered. I wish we could have lived 'happily ever after,' but that's obviously not going to happen. Still, you'll have my love forever nevertheless.

"I know that you don't particularly believe in God, but something brought us together for this short time for a reason. I know that you have come to doubt your heroism, but you are indeed, and always will be, my hero." She rose out of her chair with her eyes flashing, moved toward him, stopped a couple of feet in front of him and stared intently at him.

"I'm not feminine wily at this … all I can be is honest with how I feel."

Steve sat there unable take his eyes off of this strikingly beautiful woman in her hotel room telling him how much she loved him. His heart was pounding.

"And yes, I know you're married with three children. How do you think it makes me feel to fall head over heels for a married man? I fought it! Oh how I fought it." She spun around and walked back over to the window.

"I wish it were different," Steve managed to say softly. "But it's not, and there is nothing I can do about that." Both remained quiet for several minutes.

"Now it's time for you to go. I hope we both don't lose our jobs over this. But if we do, it was still worth it. Getting the report was good, but getting to know and love you was even better," Charlie said as she stood staring at him. She put her head in her hands. "Now I think its time for you to leave my life."

After a short time of staring at this gently sobbing woman, Steve rose out of the chair and turned to leave. Charlie dropped her hands and walked quickly over to him. "Wait. We have one last bit of unfinished business."

She reached up, threw her arms around him and gave him a long kiss on the mouth that she hoped he'd never forget. He gently put his arms around her and returned the kiss with everything he had.

She gently dropped her head against his chest and pushed her shapely body against his for several seconds. Then she turned, pulled away and walked back to the window, never turning so that he couldn't see her cry. Steve started to say something, but he stopped, turned, picked up his briefcase and walked out of her room, closing the door behind him. He reached into his pocket, took out a handkerchief and blew his nose as he walked down the hall.

CHAPTER THIRTY

It was morning now as Ellen came down from their bedroom all dressed and ready to go out for the day. She looked over at her husband sitting back in his chair and staring at the ceiling. It didn't take long for her to read his body language. "So, you have made up your mind to submit a negative report and throw your company, the country and our marriage into turmoil?"

She sat and glared across the living room at him. Her hands were held tightly together; she had an angry expression on her face that Steve had never seen before.

He sat in his favorite chair looking disheveled with uncombed hair and the beginnings of a beard, all showing that he had been up most of the night writing. He stared down at the floor from his easy chair with his hands cupped in his lap with an expressionless face. "Yea, I guess you could put it that way." He knew he was in for it, but it was probably nothing like he was going to get later from Mr. Stern when he turned in his report.

"Well, I'm not going to bore you with how I feel about it. I've already done that. I just hope that you are prepared to live with the consequences of your decision," she said angrily. Her tone dripped with sarcasm and her blue eyes flashed. Ellen was not good at hiding her feelings and she didn't try. She rose and stormed across the room.

She stopped, turned toward him and put her hands on her hips. "So now you expect us to move into an apartment in Compton or South Gate or someplace like that and try to face our new neighbors with the embarrassment of having lost your high-paying job, and the kids going to what … a public school?

"Living next door to people of all different colors? Shopping in a corner family-owned grocery store? They probably don't even have an Alpha Beta or Safeway. And how far away is Macy's?"

After some pacing, she continued, "This is what our marriage has come to!" Practically shouting now, she threw her arms up and stomped around the room occasionally glaring over at Steve.

Ellen stopped and turned to Steve. "I'm going out now to drive around and think. If you're going to work this morning you'd better shower and shave." She had calmed a bit. "You look terrible and would probably get fired if you go in looking like that."

Ellen picked up her sweater from the couch and stormed out the front door, slamming it behind her shouting back at him, "Let me know how you like living in Compton."

Steve heard tires screeching as she backed out of the driveway and sped down their street. "Consequences! What a terrible word," Steve said to himself as he got up and headed toward their bathroom for a shower and shave.

"I'm glad that the kids had already left for school before this outburst. This problem is bigger than our marriage or my job. She said let her know how I like living in Compton? She didn't say we. What does that mean?"

At 3:00 that afternoon, Steve sat at his desk staring out

his office window, vaguely hearing Louise typing furiously. She was trying to finish his report before Mr. Stern went home. Steve took out his fingernail clippers and nervously trimmed his nails again even though there was nothing left to trim.

He stood up, paced around his office, and returned to his desk. Even beyond his door, Louise sensed his nervousness and typed as fast as her arthritic figures could move. He knew that she was moving at top speed while trying to read his scribbling as best as she could.

She was accustomed to his writing after years of transcribing his reports into legible English. He was a good engineer, but engineers are not known for their ability to write or speak proper English and he was no exception.

Steve was convinced that she was the best secretary in the plant. This fact weighed heavily on him as he envisioned her losing her job along with all the others as the plant closed its doors. All this would happen because he had blown the whistle on the design flaw in their latest fighter plane.

The irony was that she was typing the report that would shut them down. This fact was not lost on her as she frantically tried to finish Steve's report. She seriously thought about throwing it all in the trashcan and going home. However, her loyalty was with her boss whom she had served for over ten years. So she kept typing as fast as she could. As she tried to concentrate on Steve's scribbling, she kept visualizing receiving her own pink slip and walking out the door along with several thousand other employees.

Louise had worked many hours of unpaid overtime sitting with Steve helping him navigate the politics of their company. She would remind him of meetings, brief him on the attendees, their foibles, their likes and dislikes, fears and hopes. Managers were amazed at how much he knew about everyone attending a meeting. He had been briefed by a genius, but only he knew who this genius was.

When he got back from one of those meetings, he would say to her, "Guess who surprised everybody with his knowledge of the issues discussed." She would stare at him with a look of fake disgust, and he would give her a big hug. She was very proud of him, but she couldn't let him know it, so she would say something like, "Oh sure, but your shirt was unbuttoned," trying to keep him humble.

"Well, no one is perfect," he would jokingly answer and quickly button the top button on his shirt. He couldn't have survived without her. Now she was writing his report that would get them both, and many more, fired!

"Consequences! Screw consequences," Steve shouted at the wall. Louise stopped typing to look up and see who her boss was talking to. She shook her head when she saw that he was alone and went back to finishing the report.

CHAPTER THIRTY-ONE

When Steve walked briskly into Mr. Stern's outer office carrying his report, he saw Janet efficiently typing away at her desk. He tried to restrain himself, but it was futile, especially as his own report was about to put him out of his job. He walked over to her desk.

"You know, I think you are a pretty woman. You just fool us with that tight hair-do Mr. Stern wants you to wear." He smiled with what he thought would be his last comments to the boss' secretary.

"No, Steve, you can't go in." Janet had ignored his not-so-funny remark, jumped out of her chair and ran toward him. He ignored her and threw open the office door to see two men sitting in comfortable chairs. They both turned toward the disturbance at the door with startled looks on their faces. One was Mr. Stern and the other was an Air Force general who Steve had seen before but whose name he couldn't remember.

Steve marched into the office with Janet running after him. The two men sitting there leaned back and both smiled. "We were just talking about you, " Mr. Stern said through his smile. Janet stopped at the door as Steve gathered his strength and marched up to the beautiful desk taking up a big part of the room. Mr. Stern waved at her that it was okay for Steve to come in.

Taking a deep breath Steve thrust out his report and slammed it down on Mr. Stern's desk. "So here it is, Mr. Big. This report may not be what you expect or want, but it is the truth as Charlie and I believe it to be." The general and Mr. Stern glanced at each other with no expression.

Steve continued. "So that you don't have to spend any time reading it, let me tell you what it says." He was on a roll now and spoke like a man who was about to lose his job and didn't care what his boss thought.

"It says that this company's badly designed wing slats caused the death of many brave and competent Air Force pilots." Steve glanced over at the general who looked curiously at this insubordinate and angry major.

"Could the design flaw have been prevented? Maybe not. But it could have been identified earlier with a little competent detective work and honest evaluation. Yea, I guess that's the big problem here. No one in power would admit that there was a problem nor was willing to take the steps to correct it. So it got worse and more people died." The two older men shifted uncomfortably in their seats.

"I know that you don't want to hear this; you've told me as much. So I assume that my usefulness to this company is over. Consequently, I have included my resignation at the beginning of the report, so that you don't have to fire me."

Mr. Stern opened the report and pulled out Steve's letter of resignation. Without expression, he read it quickly and set it down on his desk. He looked up at the angry man standing with his fists clenched and staring down at him.

Mr. Stern answered, "If that's what you want. But before you go, General Edmonds and I would like to show you something." The two men rose out of their chairs and led Steve over to the door where Janet was still standing. When they arrived in the outer room they all turned right and headed down the hall a short distance to what was apparently a new corner office with an empty secretary's desk in front of the door.

Mr. Stern opened the door and motioned Steve to go in ahead of him. Steve's jaw dropped. Here was a beautiful corner office filled with stuffed chairs, a coffee bar in the corner, bookshelves against one wall filled with the latest design books, a small meeting table in another corner and a drafting table against the remaining wall. To top it all off a set of windows framed a beautiful, if slightly smoggy view of Los Angeles in the far corner. Everyone was quiet as Steve looked around in shock. Mr. Stern finally broke in.

"This is the office of our next vice president in charge of design engineering, whoever he might be." He looked over at the general with a smile. 'He will have his own space in the executive parking lot in which to park his new company car, a key to the executive dining room and a personal private secretary.

"He will be the project engineer on our next fighter plane, the F-99, the contract for which General Edmonds here has just told me that the Air Force is awarding to us. And all the design people, including Ben, will work for the man who sits in this office. Of course this new position will require a large salary increase for whoever gets it.

"And I almost forgot. This position will require the best secretary in the company, except for Janet of course." Mr. Stern took Steve by the arm and turned him around. Steve almost fainted when he saw Louise walk through the door with her arms full of documents and personal equipment. She was followed by two workers pushing furniture dollies filled with typewriters and other secretarial gear. She had a sheepishly sly grin on her face, but said nothing as she began to unload her gear on the secretary's desk outside the office door.

"Now if we could only think of someone to fill the roll of vice president ... hmm." He put his fingers up to his chin in a mock thinking position as he glanced up to the ceiling. They all waited for Steve to say something.

"I guess ... that's my cue to apologize and retract my resignation," he said with a smile. Mr. Stern pulled Steve's resignation letter out of his pocket, tore it up and put the pieces in the wastebasket sitting by the big desk. Everyone shook hands.

"I suspect that I owe you an explanation, Steve," Mr. Stern said as he looked a little embarrassed. "You see, I was actually baiting you a bit, in effect challenging you not just to identify the slat problem and its solution, but also to come up with a negative report on our F-87. We did know what the problem was but not what caused it.

"Our second problem, in addition to identifying the cause and solution to the slat failure was that we are also looking for the best man to be our vice president of engineering. We all liked you for the job but needed confirmation that you stood for the things that would make Western Aviation a leader in the aerospace field. I know it sounds corny, but the future for this company, to which General Edmonds can testify, should be very promising. However, we are understaffed and not prepared to deal with the design and project issues that we can see down the road. You, Steve, have solved both of our problems.

"Remember, the public and the newspapers were all accusing us of white washing the problem in hopes that we wouldn't have to fix it. Nothing could have been further from the truth, but, public opinion is important to us and it was impossible to convince them until you came along.

"You'd developed an impeccable reputation both as a hero in the war and as test pilot. You were the obvious choice to 'solve' our little problem. If you'd listened to me and glossed over the problem you'd have been no value to us. Instead you told the truth in spite of the threat from me of being fired. You stood up to me as you stood up to the Luftwaffe during the war. You're the man we want for vice president of design engineering."

"And now it's my turn," General Edmonds said with a smile on his face as he reached into his pocket and pulled out a small box. He held it out and opened the hinged lid. Steve bent over and looked closely into it. His eyes popped as he saw two silver oak leaf clusters, the kind that gets pinned on uniforms. "That's right. You have been promoted to lieutenant colonel in the United States Air Force Reserve."

"Thank you, Sir," is all that Steve could think to say. They shook hands again. "Congratulations, Colonel," everyone said in unison."

"Okay, here's the plan; today is Thursday. Go home now Steve and take the long weekend to bring your family up to date. Louise will move in here tomorrow and will have your office ready to go Monday morning when you come to work. I have scheduled a meeting at 2 o'clock Monday with all your department heads. Louise can bring you up to date on them on Monday morning. Come to work ready to hit it. We've got lots to do."

Everyone turned to walk out of Steve's new office when they all came to a sudden halt. Standing in front of them leaning up against the secretary's desk in a provocative manner stood a very attractive woman with her arms folded across her chest, the top two buttons on her blouse unbuttoned and a sexy look about her. "What have we here?"

"My God. It's Janet with her hair down," Steve remarked. "Oh I know. I made a stupid remark coming into your office about how she might be a pretty woman if she would just let her hair down. I guess she's showing us that I was right. Or, she's showing us she knew it to be true all along but preferred to keep professional at work."

Janet ran her hand through her hair and turned around so that everyone could see that she actually had long bright red hair. "So, what do you think Mr. Pritchard? Do I pass muster?" Everyone laughed, as Steve's face became redder and redder. He nodded, turned and walked quickly toward the exit.

"You know, I kind of like 'Mr. Big'. Do you suppose we could put it above my door, Janet?" They were walking back to his office. She laughed as she put her red hair back into its bun. "It's strange Janet, but I've never seen you laugh before," Both Janet and Mr. Big chuckled.

CHAPTER THIRTY-TWO

Steve turned his car into his driveway, came to a stop, put on the emergency brake and pushed open the door. He took a deep breath as he stepped out of his car and looked west toward the haze-covered ocean shinning bright from the sun dipping low in the afternoon. "Wow. No fog today, and no smog living this close to the ocean," he murmured.

He had been practicing how he was going to tell Ellen about what had happened to him this afternoon. He was a little startled to see that her car was not in the driveway. "She probably put it in the garage," he thought.

He took the steps two at a time and walked into the house shouting, "Ellen, I'm home." He stood there waiting for his wife to come running in from the yard to great him with a big kiss as she had for over fifteen years. But there was only silence.

He walked slowly into the living room and was startled to see his three children sitting on the sofas looking glum. The youngest, Carolyn, had a tear running down her cheek. The other two, Matt and Jennifer, looked as if they were about to cry.

Steve didn't say anything for a moment. He was afraid to ask a question to which he didn't want an answer. He slowly moved over and sat in his favorite chair, first taking off his coat and loosening his tie. He finally took a breath and said, "So where's Mom?"

No one answered for a moment. Then his son, Matt, now fifteen and the oldest, finally said softly, "Mom's gone."

"What do you mean she's gone?" But Matt had said all he was going to for the moment.

Then Jennifer, the middle child, finally said softly,

"Today was only a half day at school, so we got home for lunch in time to watch mom, who had returned from her morning drive, pack her car and drive off."

"Didn't she say anything?"

"Oh yea, she said quite a bit." replied Matt. "She sat us down just before she left and explained it all to us. Dad, we're not moving to Compton are we? Where is Compton anyway?"

"No, Son. We're not going anywhere. What did she say about that?"

Now Carolyn who was a very mature eleven-year old added, "Mom said you were going to be fired today and we would have no place to live. She said that maybe you could get a job as a mechanic and we could afford to live in Compton or South Gate. Dad, where's Compton?"

"Okay guys, first thing, stop worrying about moving anywhere. I didn't lose my job, but I've been promoted. I'm now vice president of engineering with a big raise. Do any of you know where your mom is, so I can reach her and tell her the big news?"

The kids all looked at each other, but none said anything for a minute. "You tell him." Carolyn said to Matt.

"Never mind, I'll tell him. He'll find out sooner or later." She turned to her dad. "Mom says that you two were married too young. She was barely twenty when you married and she didn't have the opportunity to sew her wild oats, whatever that means."

Matt jumped in, "She said that some women are cut out to be wives, some to be mothers and some to be neither. She said that she loves all of us very much, but she is not sure if she is cut out to be either, at least not at this time of her life." There was a moment's silence as Steve contemplated what they were saying.

"But that doesn't answer where she went."

"Yes, Dad, we know. But there is more," Carolyn piped up. "She apparently had a high school sweetheart who none of us knew about. She didn't tell us his name, but apparently they've never forgotten each other and have been in contact. He recently lost his wife and wondered if mom was married. He got our address from the reunion rolls and the two have been writing back and forth for some time."

"But it gets worse." Now it was Matt again. "As you know, mom grew up in Seattle, and her parents moved to L.A. just after she graduated from high school which made her very unhappy. She hasn't seen this old boyfriend since she left."

"But now that is about to change." It was Jennifer this time. "There is a reunion of her old high school class scheduled in a couple of weeks, and this old boyfriend has invited her to accompany him as his date. She accepted and is headed north to Seattle as we speak."

Matt joined in. "In addition, mom spent lots of time complaining how she hates L.A. and loves Seattle. She complained about the smog here and dreams about living where it rains. I can't understand why anyone would want to live where it rains, but I think she's going to stay there after the reunion." There was quiet for a while as it all sank in.

Matt continued, "Mom loved you very much and was

very excited when you got married and then when we three came along. It all seemed to be perfect to her.

Jennifer broke in, "But as she matured, it apparently became clear to her that she was living in the wrong place, doing the wrong thing and being the wrong person. It has taken her several years to work that out, but now she has made a decision to give up everything that many women would give their eye teeth for." Jennifer was also beyond her years in understanding human nature. Steve thought she would grow up to become a psychologist.

They looked at each other without saying anything. "We all hope that mom will change her mind and come home, but, unless that happens, we are without a mother, and you are without a wife." It was Matt again who said what they were all thinking.

Carolyn got up, walked over to her father and crawled up on his lap sobbing softly. "What are we going to do, Papa?"

"Okay guys, let's think this thing through." Steve could finally speak as he ran his fingers through Carolyn's hair. "First of all, as angry and hurt as we all are, we have to respect your mom's wishes. It won't do any of us any good to mope around the house watching for her car to drive up the driveway. We have to deal with what is real.

"I have loved your mom very much and won't get over her soon, but if she wishes to be alone for the rest of her life or whatever, so be it. I presume that she stopped by our bank and withdrew our savings to live on until she gets a job." Steve had a hard time getting in touch with his feelings, especially anger, but he was learning. He stared out at their swimming pool for a couple of minutes trying to get control of himself.

"We have to live the rest of our lives with what we have. I have a great job and intend to keep it. We're not moving, but you're going to spend more time without a parent here now, and more time with each other. I'll find a nice woman to be with you when I have to work late or be out of town."

After a few minutes of thought, Steve continued, "As I look back on the past few months, I can now see things that I hadn't noticed before. I don't want to be more specific, but there were signs that I missed because I didn't want to see them. Maybe I could have prevented this if I'd been awake.

"Unfortunately, my new job is going to keep me away from home quite a bit of the time, including overnight at times. Yes, we all wish your mom were here, but that's not likely to happen, and we all need to resign ourselves to that fact." All three kids were sobbing now.

"The road of life has some major bumps in it and this is certainly one of them. Each of us will grieve in his or her own way, and that's natural. Don't be ashamed of anger and grief. There's nothing wrong with that. And remember, above all, I'm not going anywhere and will always be here for you.

There was quiet for a while, and then Jennifer spoke up. "Dad, we don't want a baby sitter or to have to count on each other. We are barely teenagers. As much as we miss mom, and always will, couldn't you find a woman that we could respect or something? Sure, we will always love our mom wherever she is, but we need two parents, not just one when we come home from school.

Steve looked up from staring at the floor with a light in his eyes. "Okay, but that's not going to be easy and you're going to have to help me select her. I won't bring home someone you don't like. Is that agreed?"

"Agreed Dad," they all said in unison trying to be more mature than they were.

Steve nodded, picked up their telephone, pulled out his address book, opened it and dialed a number.

"Yes. May I have room 517 please? " Oh Mrs. Collins has left? Did she say where she was going? No? Okay. Thank you." Steve sat the phone down and stared out at the Pacific Ocean trying to hide his disappointment.

Steve thumbed through his phone book again until he found Charlie's number in Palo Alto. He laid his phone book on the table and dialed the number. The automated lady came on saying that the number had been disconnected and there was no new number. He hung up.

Turning back to his kids, he said, "Keep your fingers crossed guys. There's lots of work to be done yet, and I'm not exactly sure where we're headed, but we're going to make it. I think that this is the time that we all have to be heroes-----"

EPILOGUE

I don't know if the design problems described in this story reflect the reality of America's primary fighter plane in the late 1940's and 1950's. However, I do know from reading authentic accounts and talking to experienced Air Force pilots that some problem did exist in some models of the F-86 causing some of them to rotate out of control. Today one can visit the air museums around the country and see the wing slats stowed along the leading edge of this magnificent Korean War era fighter plane.

However, the problem was apparently not with the slats themselves but with their deploying mechanism. It is interesting to note that many, if not all, of the modern commercial jets utilize wing slats to increase their lift during take-off and landings. One can only hope that they have solved the design problems that plagued the industry during the 40's and 50's.

I have never designed airplanes, but as an experienced aerospace and mechanical engineer, I believe that my hero's discovery could very well have identified the source of the design flaw in the deployment mechanism of the wing slats. I have never seen anything in print that identified why the slats might have deployed out of sequence, so I came up with what I think is a plausible cause and made a story out of it. Whatever was the exact cause of the wing slat's malfunction, it is seems impossible that both the manufacturer and the Air Force either didn't know about the problem or, for reasons we also do not know, did not correct it in time to prevent the death of all who died in our country's front line fighter.

Who among us would have the courage to blow the whistle revealing a deadly design flaw that would have such serious consequences on the whistle blower and on the industry? How many bridges have collapsed and cars crashed that could have been prevented because some part was not designed or built properly? As an engineer, I take our design responsibilities very seriously, but would I have the courage to do the right thing when the chips were down? I honestly don't know. Maybe. Hopefully.

In any case, my cousin, First Lieutenant James Teeslink, and his wingman did not deserve the fate to which they were subjected. Jimmie had never married and has no descendants. His parents died many years ago and his older sister, Marie, if she were alive today, would be approaching ninety. I suspect that her grandchildren and perhaps great grandchildren probably know little or nothing about their great uncle, so perhaps they will read this story and be tempted to find out more about him and his short life.

Jimmie played the guitar and had a beautiful baritone voice with which he would often serenade the officers and their wives with cowboy songs in the officers' club at McChord Air Force Base. We were told that he gave his last performance for his fellow officers and their wives the night before he was killed.

It is sad to contemplate that no one will probably ever again visit his gravesite at the federal cemetery in southeast Portland, Oregon. He gave his all for his country at age twenty-five, and there is nothing to show for his short life but the picture of a handsome young pilot climbing into the cockpit of his interceptor taken one week before his death plus a flat stone marker embedded along a beautiful green hillside at the federal cemetery on the outskirts of Portland.

AUTHOR'S BIOGRAPHY

Arthur (Art) Edwards is a retired aerospace engineer and manager who designed, built and operated large space simulation facilities at Lockheed Missiles, Sunnyvale, now Lockheed Martin, and Ford Aerospace, now Space Systems Loral in Palo Alto. He was also an adjunct professor, who taught courses in engineering, business management, organizational behavior, leadership and project management at San Jose State University, University of California, Santa Cruz and at the University of San Francisco. He has a bachelor's degree in Mechanical Engineering from University of California Berkeley, and a master's degree in Cybernetic Systems from San Jose State University.

He was a naval officer and veteran of the Korean War, serving on an attack transport in the Sea of Japan and across the Pacific in the mid 1950's transporting soldiers, marines and airmen in and out of Inchon. He left the naval reserve a few years later as a lieutenant and is now retired and lives with his ex-school administrator wife in the Gold Country of California.

While working in the aerospace industry and teaching, Mr. Edwards found time for his true love, playing timpani in the Oakland Symphony Orchestra, the Santa Cruz

Symphony, the Chapman Symphony Orchestra and the Sierra Symphony. He and his wife also sailed on San Francisco Bay in their Catalina thirty on weekends, and he was elected Commodore of the Oakland Yacht Club, Alameda, in 1991.

Now living in retirement in the foothills of the Sierra Nevada Mountains, he is working to help the homeless residents of El Dorado County by providing food, clothing and shelter to those who need it the most. Combining that experience with his love of writing, a history of the homeless community in the California foothills will hopefully be completed this fall. Please visit his company's website at www.hangtownhaven.org. for more details.

AUTHOR'S TECHNICAL PUBLICATIONS OF SPACE SIMULATION

Refurbishment of a 39-Foot Thermal Vacuum Chamber – Proceedings of the 18th Annual Space Simulation Conference – October 1994

The Evolution of Space Simulation – Proceedings of the 17th Annual Space Simulation Conference, November 1992

Fatigue Induced Cracking in Aluminum Liquid Nitrogen Tubing in 39 Foot Thermal Vacuum Test Chamber – Proceedings of the 13th Annual Space Simulation Conference, October, 1984

A Large Selectively Pumped Thermal Vacuum Test Chamber – Proceedings of the 15th Annual Meeting of The Institute of Environmental Sciences, April 1969

CPSIA information can be obtained
at www.ICGtesting.com
Printed in the USA
FSOW02n0311040217
30259FS